MOONLIGHT HEXES

M.J. CAAN

VINCI
BOOKS

By M.J. Caan

Singing Falls Witches

Vinci Books

vinci-books.com

Published by Vinci Books Ltd in 2025

1

The publisher and the author have made every effort to obtain permissions for any third party material used in this book and to comply with copyright law. Any queries in this respect should be brought to the attention of the publisher and any omissions will be corrected in future editions.

A CIP catalogue record for this book is available from the British Library.

Paperback ISBN: 9781036705619

The EU GPSR authorised representative is Logos Europe, 9 rue Nicolas Poussion, 17000 La Rochelle, France contact@logoseurope.eu

Chapter One

Torie Bliss sat on her patio, a soft, cashmere throw around her shoulders as she stared into the distance. Beyond the iron fence that wrapped her property, the large evergreens that heralded the entrance to the imposing forest of trees swayed slightly in the evening breeze. Every now and then, a sudden rustling of branches would reach her ears as squirrels leapt from one treetop to another. In the distance, owls hooted and called to one another as they organized themselves into hunting parties that frightened so many of the smaller woodland creatures that scampered about.

As the sun faded, the night air would blanket the North Carolina mountains, causing her to shiver just a little and draw her blanket tighter about her.

Something moved and stretched next to her, and she looked down to see Leo sitting on the comfortable cushion. The little dragon sensed her chill and hopped down, scampering to the fire pit that was situated not far from where Torie sat. He climbed onto the rim of the circular, stone pit, and blew orange fire down into it, causing the pit to flare to life, the tinder and logs inside bursting into flames.

Torie smiled, thankful for the warmth, and settled back, her thoughts far away as Leo climbed back onto the outdoor sofa and curled up in her lap.

She heard the back door open and close and looked over to see Elric walking towards her, carrying two glasses and a bottle of wine. He sat the bottle on the side table next to the sofa, poured the wine and handed one of the glasses to her before seating himself.

"Thank you," Torie said, lightly clinking her glass to his as he settled his body next to hers.

"I was going to ask if you wanted me to start a fire for you, but I see someone has already beat me to it."

Torie smiled, one hand stroking the dragon's back as he began to drift off to sleep in her lap.

"He has certainly come a long way," said Elric. "And it's obvious that he loves you."

Something in his voice made her look over at the were-wolf, his eyes glinting in the crackling glow of the flames as he gazed out over the landscape.

Torie reached over and took one of his hands in hers. "I know how you feel about me. you don't have to project it onto a dragon, Elric."

"I know. It's just that, you've been so quiet lately. Ever since Sable came to town. I know you need time and distance, and I'm willing to give you both; I just don't want you to ever think how I feel about you has changed."

At the mention of the she-wolf that had shown up at her housewarming party, Torie felt the corners of her mouth drop, and she shifted her weight uncomfortably. It took her a moment to realize she was squeezing Elric's hand a little harder than was necessary, and she forced herself to relax her grip.

She sighed, dropping her head back to rest on the padded back of the sofa.

"I'm sorry if I've given you the impression that I feel that way. But you're right, I needed...I need...time to process."

She wanted to add, it's not every day the man you opened your heart to tells you he has a fated mate he was preordained to be with forever.

The look in Elric's eyes told her that she didn't have to say it aloud; the wolf was almost as good at reading her as the dragon was.

"We need to talk about this, Torie," he said, rubbing the top of her hand with his thumb. "We don't have a lot of time."

"I know. It's just a lot to take in. I guess what really bothers me is that you never told me about this. We've talked about everything over the last year. We've made plans, Elric. And it never occurred to you to tell me that you're...I don't even know what to call it."

"Fated. I am fated to be with another."

She withdrew her hand from his grasp. "I hate that word. Fated." It sounded so primitive to her ears. No, primitive wasn't right; it sounded *primal.*

They had spoken very little since the housewarming party; Torie had occupied herself with unpacking the last of her personal belongings and getting her new house in order, and Elric had given her the space he instinctively knew she needed. He had spent time working with Max, his old alpha leader who was now the sheriff of the tiny community of Singing Falls.

The town had been incredibly busy of late; new supernaturals and humans alike had moved into the picturesque town perched on the side of a mountain. The scenic beauty of the mountain provided them with temperate weather that consisted of warm days and cool nights, and mostly sheltered them from severe winter storms. It had attracted a lot of interest in individuals looking for someplace away from the big cities. A place that provided a sense of community and encouraged a live and let live attitude.

The fact that it was a haven for supernatural creatures who were tired of being hunted, either by their own kind or humans, had spread among shifter clans, and many had moved to Singing Falls looking for a new start. Some humans were aware of who and what they lived among; others might have sensed something different about certain townsfolk, but they didn't ask.

Live and let live was the unspoken motto.

Max, a werewolf like Elric, had taken on the role of the town sheriff and helped to protect the town's secret when it came to the outside world. Elric had recently taken a position as a forest ranger, patrolling the higher mountain hiking trails and lake communities that were experiencing a population boom at the moment. It was perfect for him in that it allowed him to spend time outdoors where he was at his most comfortable, while simultaneously letting him keep an eye out for anything unsavory that might come down from the silver areas to the north of Singing Falls or up into town from their more savage sister city, Trinity Cove.

It was part of his wolf nature to claim a territory, and consciously or not he had claimed Singing Falls. Not the least of which was because it's where the woman he loved resided.

Unfortunately, claiming a territory wasn't the only part of his werewolf heritage that had begun to show itself.

"It is something that was arranged long before I was the man I am today," he said to her.

They had never really talked much about it, but time was growing short, and Torie sensed the urgency that played into his words. She took a deep draw of her wine and turned to face him.

"So, this woman, Sable, do you love her?"

"No, not in the way that I love you." There was no hesitancy, and that made her feel a little better at least.

"So not like you do me, but does that mean you do have *some* kind of feelings for her?"

"I would be lying if I said I did not," the wolf replied, sipping from his own glass. "But it's more like a sense of protection I feel. It is familial love, not romantic. Until I met you, I did not know there was a difference. But I always suspected there had to be more to life than just what was involved in the packs."

"Why didn't you stay with her if that was the only life you knew?"

"Because I didn't even know her. We weren't from the same pack. As a matter of fact, we were from warring packs. Our union was the first time fated mates had been found outside of our immediate pack. We were unique, and the leaders of both packs thought our union would be a way to end our territorial fight. We would be united into a single, large pack and would spread our dominance over the entire Northeast region."

"You once told me you were born and raised in the upper territories of Maine, right?"

Elric nodded. "The northern reaches of Maine are very desolate. There aren't a lot of people living up there, and almost no towns to speak of. It is so remote that what roads there are do not have names.

"The pack that Max and I are from was one of the largest in the region. We held sway of the land east of the great lake that divided the range. The other pack, the Idle Winds pack, controlled the area to the west of the lake. Of course, each pack wanted what the other had, so there was constant fighting among them. It wasn't for me."

He stopped and drank more wine, reaching over to lazily pet Leo as he stretched in his sleep.

"At what age did you know you were fated to someone?" Torie asked.

"Age for werewolves is not the same as what it is for humans. Being a beta, I didn't even know it was possible to have a fated mate; typically, that is reserved for alphas."

"Like Max," Torie said.

Elric nodded. "Yes, the alphas are fated, but anyone below that on the social scale would typically just end up with whomever they hit it off with. Kind of like humans in that regard."

"Elric, what happened with Max then? Why isn't he with his mate?"

"She was killed in a brutal encounter with the Idle Winds pack. Things were getting heated between our packs, and one day, Max thought it would be a good idea to do some scouting in an area where our territories overlapped. It wasn't unheard of, that wolves can have certain spots that you would consider no-man's land. An area that any who were brave enough could enter.

"He had caught the scent of some game and was tracking it, along with Atema, his mate. They were ambushed. He escaped, but she…well, Max has never forgiven himself for that. I think that is part of the reason he was so willing to leave the pack with me and head south until we eventually came across Trinity Cove. And well, you know everything that has happened with us since then."

"You said that was part of the reason he left. What was the other?"

Elric took a deep breath and remained quiet for a moment. Torie stood and topped up their drinks, waiting for him to continue.

"It was around that time that I felt the call of my mate. I am not really sure how to explain it. It's like a scent on the breeze that you experience with all of your senses at once. It's a longing that pulls at you, and the more you ignore it, the harder it yanks. Until finally, you head off alone, into the woods, to find the source. That's what I did. Left my pack for a couple of days until I had hiked far into the ranges above the lakes.

"And that was when I met Sable. She had felt the pull as well. When two fated mates find one another, it can be quick, because you are both born into the same pack. But with us, we were pulled together far away from the eyes of our packs. I suppose it would have been fine had we settled down where we were, starting our own pack in an unmarked territory. But we decided not to do that. We were strangers to one another and were each wary of the other."

"So, did the two of you…?" Torie couldn't bring herself to finish the sentence.

"Mate? No, we did not. We resisted the urge, because we both knew that once we did that, the bond between us could only be separated by death."

His voice trailed off, and Torie could tell that something had registered on his supernatural senses. Leo lifted his head off her lap, his snout quivering in the flickering light as his body began to vibrate slightly.

"What is it?" she said to Elric.

Then she saw it; a shadow separated from the darkness of the trees and sprinted towards her property.

She stood quickly, calling up her magic to hold at the ready until Elric held out a hand, letting her know it was okay. In the blink of an eye, the shadow reached her retaining wall and, leaping high into the air, cleared it and the iron fence atop the rock wall, before casually walking up to the fire.

"Hello, Elion," said Elric. "You really should announce yourself better."

"Forgive me, but there was little time." He nodded to Torie and then turned to face Elric. "He has dispatched scouts, and I believe one of them picked up Sable's scent a few miles south of here."

Elric stiffened, causing a sudden spike in Torie's adrenaline.

"What are you talking about?" she said, "And who dispatched scouts?"

"You haven't told her?" said Elion.

"We were just getting to that part," replied Elric.

Torie looked at both supernaturals, arching her eyebrows in expectation. "Tell me what?"

Elric turned to her. "The big reason Max left the pack was because of the ruler of the Idle Winds pack. In retribution for the death of his fated one, Max killed the fated of their alpha. That alpha was his brother."

Chapter Two

Torie was shocked at the revelation and didn't know what to say. She stared hard at Elric, who could only swallow hard, taking a long drink from his glass.

"Were you a part of that?" asked Torie.

"No. I did not know what he had done until it was too late. After that, there was nothing more Max could do. He had to run. Staying with the pack would have meant all-out war, and as we were no match for the size of his brother's pack, it would have meant certain death for everyone.

"By running, it removed the need for confrontation. I, being Max's second, left with him. That created a second problem. It meant Sable had no fated mate. No one knew I was to be her mate, so Max's brother chose her to become his new mate. He lied about there being a fated bond between them and forced her to be his. I assume she ran as well at some point. We ended up in Trinity Cove, and apparently, so did Sable." He looked at Elion, and the vampire could only nod.

"She was drawn to Trinity Cove because you were

here," Elion said. "She tried to blend in with the community over the past year. Even once you were gone, she felt like she had found a place where she could start over again, far from the watchful eyes of a demanding pack."

"So what, then the two of you met and fell in love?" asked Torie.

"Yes," Elion said matter-of-factly. "That is exactly what happened."

"And you had no idea she was here?" Torie turned to Elric.

"No. I had already established myself here by the time she arrived. We only found out when I met up with Elion to help us with Leo. He told Max and I that Sable was in town, and that they had become involved."

"Is that why you stayed here?" asked Torie. "Is that what you wanted all along? Someone to break the fated bond between Elric and Sable?"

Elion nodded, though he could not meet Torie's gaze.

"We don't even know if it is possible," he said. "The few witches we knew back in Trinity Cove would not attempt it; they had no interest in involving themselves in something that could be considered an act of war with a large pack of werewolves."

"So then, what makes you think I would try it?"

Elion looked from her to Elric and back again. "Because you have as vested an interest in this as I do. As long as Elric is bonded to Sable, then neither of them is completely free of the other."

Torie didn't say anything, her heart racing and her mind swirling with thoughts. She didn't know how to feel. She picked up her glass and slowly walked to the edge of the deck, looking out. Elric moved to stand beside her and placed a tentative hand on her shoulder. He felt her body tense in response and let it drop to his side.

"Elion, can you give us some space please?" Elric said.

The vampire hesitated, then nodded. "Of course." He disappeared into the house, leaving them alone in the flickering light of the fire.

Silence, punctuated by the far-off sound of frogs and the occasional hoot of an owl, seemed more pervasive than the darkness that had crept across the grounds before them.

"Why didn't you tell me, Elric?"

The big wolf sighed. "Because I didn't want to think about it. By the time I realized the true depth of my feelings for you, I thought it was too late."

"No, that was exactly when you should have told me."

"I didn't know what it meant myself. I thought that with distance and time, the bond would fade. I'm no alpha; I didn't have the right to a fated mate. I thought it couldn't be true, that maybe I had somehow misread the signs."

Torie spun to face him, her face wet as she fought back tears. "And what about Sable? Do you think she felt the same way? Why did she follow you here if she didn't feel something?"

"I don't know, Torie. I can't tell you what's in her mind or why she fled the pack. I can only tell you what I felt. And what I didn't feel." He reached out and gently wiped at her tears with his thumb. "What I didn't feel was love. Deep down, I knew that no matter what, I would never feel for Sable the way you're supposed to feel for the one you love with all your heart and soul. I think I knew that I was destined for someone else." He leaned in and kissed her on the forehead, his lips lingering. "But now I do. And I am terrified of losing that."

Torie took his hand in hers and kissed it.

"I never meant to make you angry, Torie."

"I'm not angry. Just a little sad." *And that feels worse than anger right now.*

"So, what should we do?" he asked. "I am not going to have you do anything you are uncomfortable with. I made this mess. I'm fine taking my lumps and cleaning it up the hard way."

"What is the hard way?"

"Well, at some point, Arin will find Sable. And once he's in Trinity Cove, he will realize that Max and I are here as well. He'll see it as an opportunity to get revenge on Max, take out me, and unite the two Northeast packs under his one rule."

"I can see why he would be after Max, but why would he want to kill you? It's not like you even want to be with Sable."

"Because wolves mate for life. The only way to force Sable into a new fated mate bond would be to kill her existing mate."

"Christ. You think he would actually kill you over a misplaced love? Maybe even his own brother?"

Elric nodded. "There is a strong sense of family with wolves, but it is not the same as with human siblings. Both Max and Arin were born alphas. That's almost unheard of among werewolves. They fought constantly as children, until finally, their father kicked them both out of his pack and they were each forced to create their own. Each moved to a different side of the great lake and began to build their tribe. The result…well, you know what has happened since then.

"There is still a great animosity between them, and Arin knows this is his chance to take power. Whoever rose to take

Max's place in our old pack will not stand a chance against Arin."

"So why not just take that person out and take over the packs?"

"Because the true leader will always be Max. As long as he's alive, there is always a chance he could return and cause trouble for Arin. Plus, as long as Max lives, Arin will never have the complete, slavish loyalty that he craves from everyone around him. He has to kill Max to cement his place.

"And believe me. He will kill him, without hesitation."

"God, this is all so awful. I can't say that I understand any of it, but I'm not going to stand around and watch you get killed in some crazed, Shakespearean-werewolf drama."

"There is one other thing," Elric said, his voice low. "The wolves aren't the only problem we may have to contend with. The vampires undoubtedly know about Elion and Sable by now."

"So? What do they care?"

"The union of a werewolf and a vampire is considered unnatural. It's never happened before, and the vampires are not going to be happy about it."

"So, you're saying that if the bond between you and Sable isn't broken, it results in a lot of killing. If it is broken, and she and Elion can hook up, it results in a lot of killing? Great."

"This is all more than should have been dropped in your lap. This is my fault."

"No, it isn't, and don't think that way. But at least now I think I know why no other witches would take this on."

Elric nodded. "They know the history between werewolves and vampires and were not willing to step into that."

Torie sensed there was more to that story, but she wasn't

ready to hear it. She was tired; the emotional rollercoaster she had just rode had worn her down. She needed rest and time to process.

"Come on, let's go to bed," she said. "We can call Jasmin tomorrow and talk this all through. Hey, I didn't ask, where is Sable staying?"

"She is at the Wandering Brook bed and breakfast in town."

Torie nodded. That was a good location. It was run by a fox shifter named Nora, and it wasn't far from the police station, so Max could help keep an eye on things as needed.

They walked through the kitchen, placing their wine glasses in the deep farmhouse sink, and found Elion sitting next to the fireplace in the great room.

"I'm going to talk to Jasmin tomorrow to see what we can do," said Torie.

The vampire looked up in surprise.

"I had expected you to say no. Not that I would blame you."

"Well, I'm not making any promises; so, don't get your hopes up. But I'll do what I can to help."

Torie had hoped the wine would help her sleep, but it had had the opposite effect on her. She lay there, alternating between staring at the ceiling and staring at the man she had come to love.

And he loved her. She knew that beyond a shadow of a doubt; but still, there was so much about the supernatural she didn't understand. What if having Sable this close to them could trigger something in Elric? Would he go back to her? Is the bond between fated mates stronger than human love?

She reached over and stroked his hair, smiling as he mumbled in his sleep and scooted his body closer to hers.

She felt tears building up. She had never felt anything like this before, and she knew that at this point in her life, she probably never would again.

This was something she wanted. Something she couldn't bear the thought of losing.

Something she wouldn't lose.

Maybe she couldn't break the bond between her beloved and the she-wolf, at least not without Jasmin's help, but maybe she could weaken it?

Her brow furrowed as she mulled that thought over in her head. Elric was obviously torn by what needed to be done, so this would be her way of offering him some solace in the matter. And she wouldn't tell him about it. It could be something she could do that would just live in the background, right?

No harm, no foul.

She thought for a moment and then closed her eyes, placing one hand lightly on Elric's forehead.

> *"By the powers of the moon, and blessed ides,*
> *let me be the only one, in this man's eyes.*
> *Let chains that were tight, now stretch thin,*
> *to grant free will to both wolves and men."*

She caught herself holding her breath as she watched for any signs that her spell had worked. But what exactly would happen? Finally, she let out a breath and realized there might be no way of knowing if the spell even worked. It had been a good thought, but obviously she was way out of her league with the kind of magic needed for this, so she curled up against Elric, pulled the covers around her, and feel into a deep sleep.

The next morning, Jasmin was sitting at the large kitchen island, a box of fresh scones sitting in front of her while the aroma of coffee filled the room.

"Absolutely not. No way," she said, her eyes narrowing at Torie, who blinked wide eyes at her.

"Well, don't you think it's something we should consider? Or at least talk about?"

"It sounds like it's something you've already considered. You're just looking for me to agree with you."

Torie realized she wasn't wrong. Had she already made up her mind and just assumed her friend would go along with it? She briefly considered telling Jasmin about the spell she attempted but realized there was no need. Especially if it didn't work. Jasmin would probably just scold her for being reckless.

When Sable had told them what was going on at Torie's housewarming party, Jasmin had been very empathetic, and Torie reminded her of that.

"Well, what was I going to say in the moment? I mean, I feel for the girl, but this is not something we need to get into."

"That's the same thing the witches in Trinity Cove told them. Am I missing something here? We have a friend who needs our help, and we are just going to turn our backs on them?"

Jasmin gave her a steely look and started to say something but then held her tongue.

"What? Go ahead, you can say whatever you want. Help me understand."

Jasmin bit the inside of her lip, and Torie could tell she was choosing her words carefully.

"Torie, I think that you are thinking with your heart and not your head. We don't know this werewolf. You are looking at this from the point of view of a woman who wants to help her boyfriend. And that by helping him, it ultimately helps you because it will make you feel better in your relationship with said boyfriend."

Torie didn't say anything but could feel a blush of crimson creeping up her neck and spreading to her cheeks.

"It's not that simple," she said. "The key player in this is Max's brother. He wants to kill Max, assume his role as alpha of their old pack. He will also kill Elric because he supported Max *and* because it will force Sable to then choose another fated mate. And guess who Max's brother wants that mate to be?"

Jasmin chewed on a scone as she regarded her friend.

"Jasmin, Max's own brother is going to kill him. We can't just stand by and watch."

Torie could practically read Jasmin's mind. She didn't need to say what was so obvious between them.

Jasmin sighed. "And of course, if anyone knows what it's like to have a sibling try to kill them, it's me."

"And just like I would never stand by and let that happen, I can't let it happen to Max either. And yes, if I'm being honest, I am thinking about myself as well. I love Elric and I don't want to lose him. In any way. I think if we don't do anything, then he's going to go on the run again. His loyalty to Max is beyond stubborn I think."

Jasmin huffed. "It isn't loyalty that would make him run, silly. If he were to take off it's to protect you. Werewolves are particularly vicious when it comes to vengeance on someone who has turned their backs on their own kind. If this wolf is willing to kill his own brother, what do you think he would do to someone else who crosses his path?"

Torie hadn't considered that. She only knew werewolves from her exposure to Elric and Max. Elric was so kind and gentle. Imagining him in some kind of bloodlust rage was not something she could picture.

"Tell you what," said Jasmin. "I'll consider this, but I want you to consider something for me as well."

Torie frowned. "Anything. You know that."

"Well, first wait to hear what it is. Come on, we're meeting Fionna at Jim's Bakery. She's a part of this as well."

Torie wasn't sure why her friend was being so vague, but she gathered her purse and followed her out the door.

Chapter Three

The inside of the bar known as Push Dagger, was dark and dank. The place smelled of mildew and vomit that had been washed away with only water. There was a juke box in the far corner that played a mix of eighties country and rock; at least when it worked that was what it played. The plastic bubble that shielded it from the open air was cracked in multiple places and dried blood was caked to the edge of it.

Like the men and women that frequented Push Dagger, the old juke box had seen better days.

A myriad of eyes looked up at the band of men that entered, taking them in with a quick, practiced sweep. Nostrils flared as the strangers' scents were pulled in by many of the bar patrons as well. Most went back to their drinks, or the intimate conversations they were engaged in. A few watched the band of men closely, giving them their full attention.

Arin Long Tooth stopped in the middle of the bar space, his men filing in around him. He tilted his head back and took a deep snort of the air, sorting the patrons by type and rank.

There were mostly shifters in the bar. He recognized what most of them were, but there were a couple who smelled of an animal he wasn't familiar with. There were a couple of banshees and a vampire that scurried out the back as soon as they walked in. Luckily, there were no humans to be found in the space.

Arin drew himself to his full impressive height. He was a massive man by all standards; over six and a half feet tall, pushing two hundred and sixty pounds of pure muscle. His eyes glinted in the dim light, and he let out a low feral growl.

A hush fell over the bar as everyone looked at him.

"I'm looking for a lost member of my pack," he said. "A woman by the name of Sable. Anyone here know her?"

Silence was the only answer he received as everyone went back to their business, ignoring the big werewolf. He growled again, feeling the shift about to come over him. These creatures needed to know who he was and understand that he wasn't someone to be ignored.

Before he could transform, a slight figure in a black hooded jacket stood up from the bar.

"I know who you're talking about," she said. "Calm yourself and have a seat. Let's talk."

Arin took in the tiny figure with more than just his eyes. She had no scent that he could discern, and that bothered him for some reason.

He turned to his beta. "Take the men and wait outside for me."

The beta looked at him questioningly, his eyes flitting from Arin to the smaller figure at the bar and back.

"The men are comfortable in here," he replied. "They might like a beer after the trek we just had."

Arin's eyes flashed a dangerous yellow and a rumble built in his chest.

"The men will be comfortable where I say they will be. And right now, I need them and you outside. Now go and wait for me until I come out."

The beta hesitated a brief moment before nodding and turning to the men. He motioned for them to follow him, and they filed out of the bar into the night.

Arin approached the bar and sat down next to the woman who had spoken up.

"I'm waiting," he said.

The woman barked a laugh. "Rather rude of your beta, don't you think? Has he always questioned you like that?"

Arin was taken aback but refused to acknowledge the question. The truth was, he was shocked at his beta's gall. Something was changing with him; it was subtle, but Arin could sense it.

"Oh well, not my problem," said the woman, taking a draw from her beer. "But you mentioned someone named Sable. I saw her. She's been here in Trinity Cove for a while. Or she was. Hot footed it out of here a few days ago with another…man."

Something about the way she said 'man' triggered a twitch in Arin. "What man? Where was she going?"

The woman shrugged. "I don't know who he was. But they were in a hurry. I can guess where she was going though, based on what she was looking for here."

Arin didn't speak. He was getting tired of this tiny person and had to rein in his wolf from biting her head off.

"She was asking around for witches here in town. Something about wanting them to break a bond she had or something like that. No witch would do it however, so my bet is she caught wind of a different breed of witch that lives up in Singing Falls. I'm betting she headed there to get them to do the deed."

Arin stiffened. His mind was spinning as he had an idea of who the other man was. He couldn't imagine why she might want her bond broken, and truthfully, he didn't care.

He knew who she was with, and it made his blood boil.

"Where is this Singing Falls?" he asked. "And what kind of supernaturals live there? Is it a town of darkness like this one?"

"Oh no. There are no towns like this one," she replied. "I can answer all your questions if you'll do something for me."

"What's that?"

"Take me with you."

He regarded the woman, not quite sure what to make of her request. "We need to travel fast. And we aren't babysitting anyone once we get there."

"Oh, trust me, I can keep up with you. And you needn't worry about taking care of me. If anything, I can help watch your back. From the witches up there. And maybe even your own little beta. Something new is in the air it seems. Shifters are acting…weird."

Arin looked at her, still unwilling to acknowledge what she was hinting at.

"You can come with me. But my business there is not pretty. Don't try to stop me or get in my way."

She turned to face him, her face twisting into a dark grin.

"Why, I wouldn't think of it. Besides, I have my own ugly business there as well."

Chapter Four

The bakery was all but deserted as the two of them entered. They found Fionna sitting in their usual spot; the large leather chairs that sat in front of the stone fireplace.

The squirrel shifter stood up and greeted her two friends with a hug.

"I ordered a round of elderberry muffins and two French presses for us," she said as the two witches settled into the chairs beside her.

Her eyes were sparkling and had that gleam that could only mean she was extremely excited about something.

"So, what's going on?" Torie asked.

"Well," said Jasmin, "look around you. Don't you just love this place?"

Torie looked around, taking in the space. There was nothing different about it; tables for two were arranged along one of the back walls. Small leather loveseats and chairs flanking gaming tables were dotted throughout the room as well. Everything was laid out in a way that invited a single person to sit and read or work on a laptop; or groups could gather to discuss the latest book they were reading or spread out and work on the latest project they might be knitting. It was a comfortable space that felt open and inviting, but never crowded. All the while, the smell of fresh baked bread, pastries of all kinds, and some of the best coffee in town, enveloped you like a cherished old blanket.

"Yes, I do love this place," Torie replied. "It was one of the first places you brought me to when I moved to town, and I fell head over heels for it. Though I will say it took me a lot longer to shed those extra pounds I put on from all these pastries than it would have taken me twenty years ago."

"Oh nonsense," said Fionna. "You look amazing. And I'm glad to see you're embracing that silver streak. It's very becoming on you."

At the mention of the stripe through her hair, Torie ran her fingers through it subconsciously, still not sure how she felt about it. Their encounter with Jasmin's treacherous sister had resulted in this, and nothing had worked to remove it. The fact that Fionna was complimenting her on it felt nice, but it also felt like she was being buttered up more than the breakfast biscuits the bakery was also known for.

"Thank you, Fionna. That means a lot. And can I just say that I would kill for your figure."

Fionna was blessed with a shifter's high metabolism that let her pretty much eat anything she wanted, whenever she wanted, and she never gained an ounce. Her figure was as lithe as a dancer's, and the shifter never seemed to run out of energy.

"Well, I think we can all agree that it's a beautiful bakery," said Jasmin, looking around.

Torie creased her brow. "Where is everyone? By now there should be a line out the door."

"So that's what I wanted to talk to you about," said Jasmin, just as their coffee arrived.

Typically, they would have heard their name called and then gone to the counter to pick up their order, but this time, Torie looked up to see Jim bringing it directly to them.

She was more than a little startled to see the owner serving them, but she thanked him profusely as he sat it down on the small coffee table next to their elderberry muffins.

"Well, have you...said anything?" he asked with a smile.

"Not yet," said Jasmin. "Give us a few, please."

Jim nodded and walked away, disappearing through an open door behind the counter.

"Jasmin, what's going on?" Torie asked again.

"The place is empty because it's closed today," said Jasmin. "Jim was kind enough to let us meet here to talk about something." She poured herself a cup of coffee and then one for Torie and Fionna before continuing. "He's selling this bakery, Torie, and moving down to Florida."

"What? Why?" asked Torie, putting down the cup she had just picked up.

"He's tired," said Fionna. "He's been here for thirty years and is ready to retire. It took a lot out of him when that golem caused a fight here amongst shifters. He just doesn't have the strength to keep going. So, he's selling and moving on."

"Okay, wow. I can understand that I guess. But what happens to this place?" Torie asked.

Fionna and Jasmin exchanged excited looks.

"Well, we were thinking that maybe we could buy it from him. Take it over," said Jasmin.

Torie was shocked as she regarded her friends.

Fionna piped up, her words practically tripping over themselves in excitement. "It would be a great opportunity for us. Well, for you I mean. I don't have any money so I can't help. At least not the kind of money you witches have; but I promise I would work day and night here and do anything you needed to make this place a success."

"Think about it, Torie. This bakery is a landmark here in Singing Falls. It's already established. We could make a few upgrades, maybe expand the lunch menu a little. And we could apply for a wine license."

"How long have you two known about this?" asked Torie.

"We just found out right before your housewarming party. And after tasting that amazing cake you made for Fionna's birthday, I knew this would be right up your alley. That cake needs to be available to the world, Torie. It was that good."

"Glen is still raving about it," added Fionna. "Just think, you could add your touch to the creations this place is known for."

Torie held up her hand.

"You don't have to sell me on this; you had me at wine."

Fionna jumped to her feet, clapping her hands rapidly. "This is going to be so awesome! I can't wait!"

"So, I take it this squealing means that we have a deal?" asked Jim, his voice booming from the back of the bakery.

"I'll have my lawyer start pulling up the paperwork," said Jasmin. "But yes, we have a deal."

The group of friends raised their coffee mugs and clinked them together.

"To something old becoming our something new," said Jasmin.

"And now, can we talk about our other issue?" said Torie.

Jasmin sighed. "I suppose we need to."

"What issue is that?" asked Fionna.

Torie recounted everything to her, ending with her conversation with Jasmin just before heading over to the bakery.

"So, Fionna, what do you think?" asked Jasmin.

"That's easy. Of course we help them. And by *we* I mean you two." She didn't hesitate with her answer.

"Wait, so you don't see anything wrong with attempting this?" Jasmin pressed

"Oh, I see all kinds of wrong," the squirrel shifter answered. "I can see all kinds of horrible things happening as a result of meddling in a feud between two werewolf packs. Most of those wrong things involving blood."

"And yet you still support this?" Jasmin demanded.

"Max is our friend. Elric is our friend. He's in love with our bestie here. They are asking for help, so…we give them that help. As annoying as Max may be, we can't let him be killed by his own brother. And we certainly can't let Elric go on the run, breaking Torie's heart. Are there risks? Yes. But that doesn't mean we turn our backs on the ones we love."

No one said anything for a full minute. Torie could feel her eyes welling up at her friend's words.

"Fionna, what risks do you see in particular?"

"My biggest fear is turning this town into a new Trinity Cove. Minus the full-time darkness. That place is vicious, and I don't want that kind of atmosphere spilling over to Singing Falls. But that's what you get when you mess around with werewolves. There's a reason they were never welcome here, prior to Max and Elric. Vampires too, while we're talking about it; I still have mixed feelings about Elion being here."

"Well, we have no idea if what Sable is asking for can be done," said Jasmin. "I know nothing about the fated mate bond. We can't put all our eggs into the one basket of breaking that bond. We need to have a plan B in place, so this town doesn't become a war zone."

Torie's eyes widened. "Wait, does this mean you're saying yes?"

Jasmin rolled her eyes in response. "You had me at Torie's broken heart."

"Looks like we have a lot to do," said Torie.

Jim walked up to the ladies and offered to refill their French presses and clear away the dishes.

"You know, I couldn't help but overhear what you ladies were talking about. I've been around this town a long time, and I have to say I'm glad I'm getting out of here before this starts." He gathered their things and turned to walk away before spinning back around. "You know, one thing you might want to look into is this town's founding covenant as a sanctuary hamlet. When Singing Falls was first founded, there was an agreement forged by humans and shifters alike that all would be safe here, because anyone that sought refuge could not be harmed by anyone else through an act of violence. It's part of the bylaws."

"Seriously? That is incredible," said Jasmin. "I had no idea. Where would we go to find out more about this?"

Jim twisted his jaw to one side, scratching at the stubble on his cheeks.

"I'd say start with Alma Condos, the town librarian. That woman is old as the dirt these buildings are built on, but she's whip-smart and probably has access to the town accords. If anyone knows, it will be her."

They turned to one another as he left, their eyes bright with excitement.

"You know what this means?" said Torie. "If no one is allowed to spill blood in this town, then maybe that opens another door for us."

"What other door is that?" asked Jasmin.

"Diplomacy. Maybe we can negotiate something between Max and his brother, Arin. A peace treaty if you will."

Fionna's look told them how skeptical she was of Torie's words.

"You've obviously never met any other werewolves besides Elric and Max. They aren't exactly known for their peaceful ways. And I am born and raised in this town, and I have never heard of these accords Jim mentioned. And even if they do exist, they haven't exactly done anything to stop bloodshed. I mean, Arnold went on a killing spree and murdered a bunch of shifters, and nothing happened to him."

Torie sank back in the chair at the mention of the vampire who had been responsible for collecting shifter organs for his warlock boss before they were able to put a stop to that.

"You're right," said Jasmin. "Plus, my sister and daughter were able to do a lot of damage here as well without a lot of repercussions. We need to find out what that librarian knows."

She and Torie stood up, gathering their things. When Fionna didn't rise to join them, they turned, giving her a questioning look.

"Fionna, you coming?" asked Jasmin.

She shook her head. "No, you guys go ahead. I want to go talk to Jim. I want to start learning as much as possible about the running of this place."

"You sure?" asked Torie. "Is something bothering you? You seem a little off all of a sudden."

Fionna looked around, fidgeting with the closure on the small clutch she carried with her.

Before she could answer, Max and Elric burst into the room, zeroing in on the group of women.

"Hey, guys," said Jasmin. "What's going on?"

Elric seemed particularly on edge.

"I was up on the north ridge, patrolling the area, and I came across a scent. Werewolf scent. There is a scout somewhere in the woods north of here. And it's a member of the Idle Winds pack. That means Arin can't be too far behind."

No one said anything. A million thoughts rushed through Torie's mind.

"What do we do?" she asked.

"We need to get to the librarian to find out what can and can't be upheld by the founding covenants. If they even exist," said Jasmin.

"We need to go find that wolf that's prowling around the outskirts of town," said Max. "If he's a scout and picks up Sable's scent..."

"You handle that," said Elric. "I'm going to find Sable and make sure she knows to stay low."

"Wait," said Torie as the two wolves turned to leave the room. "You can't go after a werewolf alone. I'll go with Max."

"Trust me, I can handle myself," the sheriff said.

"I have no doubt. But what if that scout isn't alone? And I hate to say it, but you're not at one hundred percent." She pointed to her eyes, reminding the wolf that he lacked one of his own.

"Absolutely not," said Elric. "You're not going up there."

"I am and that's final," said Torie. "You go check on... Sable. Make sure she stays safe. For all we know, there could be more of those wolves already in town. I wouldn't know them if I saw one, but you would. It makes sense that you stay with her, and I go with Max. Jasmin, you handle the work with the librarian."

Reluctantly, they all agreed with the plan and split off.

Torie accompanied Max to his big, police SUV and climbed into the passenger seat. She felt more than a little distracted. She was about to face an unknown werewolf in the woods. But for some reason, that didn't weigh anywhere near as heavily in the back of her mind as another thought.

That thought being, the man she loved was off to meet up with his fated mate.

Chapter Five

Jasmin eased her car into the parking lot behind the town library. There were only a few other cars there, so she knew she wouldn't have to compete for the librarian's attention, which should make it a lot easier to get in and out with the information she needed.

The library itself was a large stone and stucco Tudor-style building that had once served as a private residence for a wealthy logging magnate whose family had settled in Singing Falls. It had fallen into serious disrepair after being abandoned by the sole remaining family member decades prior. A wealthy, anonymous benefactor had purchased it, rehabbed the building, and gifted it to the town with the express purpose of it becoming a public library.

Stepping through the large, double doors into the cool interior, Jasmin breathed in the unique scent of old books. The heavy, musky air took her back to her childhood growing up in the mountains of West Virginia where the library was her one escape from a harsh life. It's where she had discovered there was a big world outside of the coal mines she was determined to one day leave.

There was a small arts gallery that spotlighted local artists just past the entry to the building. From there, Jasmin walked through a small hall that opened to the front desk where a tall, thin woman with graying hair pulled back into a ponytail stood, her attention focused on a computer. When Jasmin approached, she could see that the woman was older than she appeared from a distance. Deep lines around her lips and eyes showed that she had spent her life in the sun, laughing and smiling. Her Mediterranean skin shone under the ambient overhead lighting.

"May I help you?" she asked before Jasmin could speak. She looked up and smiled, her amber eyes glinting in welcome.

"Hello, I'm looking for a Ms. Alma Condos."

The woman nodded, politely. "I'm Alma. How can I help you?"

"It's very nice to meet you, Ms. Condos—"

The librarian held up a hand. "Please, call me Alma."

"Alma. My name is Jasmin, and I was wondering if you could help me with some research I'm doing on Singing Falls. Jim at the bakery said you would be the one to ask about it."

Alma cocked her head to one side just a little, and her smile became a little more pinched.

"Jim, huh? He doesn't typically refer just anyone to me for questions. I assume this must be something very...particular you are interested in?"

Jasmin looked over Alma's shoulder into the library proper section of the building. There appeared to be only one other person in the room, a young girl that sat at a small table in the far corner of the room, buried in a book that looked to be almost as big as she was.

"Oh, that's just little Maura Kinsley. She likes to read those ancient Greek mythology stories. She gets lost in those books. She won't hear anything we need to speak about."

Jasmin nodded, looking back to the older woman.

"I need to know about the articles or covenants that were declared when Singing Falls was founded. Particularly, the ones that declare this to be a sanctuary location for all supernaturals." She glanced again at little Maura before lowering her voice even more and continuing. "Specifically, any references to werewolves."

Alma regarded the witch momentarily, before motioning for her to come around the counter.

Jasmin followed her towards a set of staircases that led to the second floor of the library. Before they ascended the steps, Alma leaned around the wall and called out.

"Maura, dear, I'm heading upstairs to help this nice lady. Call out if you need something, and remember, don't leave the building until your mother comes back to pick you up, okay?"

The child mumbled something in response that made Alma smile.

"Such a sweet child," she said, leading Jasmin up the stairs.

They reached a landing that led to a completely open floor with row upon row of shelves containing book after book. Walking down the first row, Alma led her to a room that sat at the back of the space. She flicked on an overhead light that revealed a large conference table with desk lamps and a couple of hardwired computers facing one another at the end of the table. On the walls were deeper shelving units that held various rolled-up documents and large, folded maps.

Alma moved to a wall at the very back of the room that had a wall safe built into it. Reaching into the pocket of a smock she wore, she retrieved a key and inserted it into the locking mechanism to open the box. Before she reached in, she withdrew a set of white gloves from her smock and donned them.

Only then did she take two rolled pieces of parchment from the safe box and place them gingerly onto the conference table.

"This is our research room," she said, carefully unrolling the scrolls and gently pressing them flat. "You can find anything and everything about Singing Falls from those maps and documents on the walls. Everything except what you are asking about. That information is only in these scrolls." She looked up, giving Jasmin a hard look. "I take it you're one of Singing Falls more *special* members of the community?"

Jasmin hesitated, but something told her that if she wanted to get as much information out of Alma as possible, she had to be forthcoming herself.

"Yes, that's correct. I'm a witch."

Alma's eyes went wide in pleasant surprise. "Oh, excellent. Yes, I have heard of you. You and your friend who just moved to town. You two have been very busy from what I've heard."

Jasmin wasn't sure if she wanted to know the woman's sources, so she didn't ask. Instead, she turned her attention to the parchment scrolls laid out in front of her, reaching gingerly for the document. Alma stopped her before she could touch them.

"Here, wear these," the librarian said, reaching into her

smock for a second set of gloves. "They are very fragile and there is no digital copy in existence."

Jasmin tugged the gloves on and then set about studying the parchments. They looked like articles of incorporation, including various amendments to town charters that spelled out the foundation of Singing Falls.

"So, I take it you are familiar with the community of supernatural beings here in Singing Falls?" she said, still studying the articles.

"Oh yes. When you've been in a place as long as I have, you get to know all the comings and goings of this town."

Jasmin looked up, opening her mouth to say something, but not quite sure how to voice it.

Turned out, she didn't have to say it aloud. Alma smiled at her.

"No, I am not a member of that community. I am as human as they come."

Jasmin smiled. "That wasn't really any of my business, but thank you for telling me."

"Can I just say that I think it's amazing what you and your friends are doing for this town. You're taking an interest in the well-being of the citizens here, and in doing so, you're inspiring others to be more…open, about their lives. Why, if I were ten years younger, I might just decide to join you on some adventures. Okay, maybe a little more than ten years."

Jasmin chuckled. "Age ain't nothing but a number, sister. I'm no spring chicken, but I feel better now than ever. If there is an adventure you want to have, I say go get it. But trust me, hanging around with me, Torie and Fionna is not what you would want to do."

Alma's smile froze in place and her body grew slightly stiffer.

"Fionna? I used to know a girl named Fionna. She was a squirrel shifter."

"Yes, that's her," said Jasmin, looking up. "How do you know her?"

"It's a small town, dear. I'm a lifelong resident, so I know just about everyone. I haven't seen her in a while, other than passing in town."

A sadness crept into her voice that caused Jasmin to give her a questioning look. Before she could ask anything, Alma quickly moved on to another subject.

"So, werewolves, huh? Nasty creatures, those. But I do hear that we have a couple in our midst who have turned out to be rather standup fellas. But I suppose you already know that, right?"

"Yes, I do. And you are correct. They are a couple of very stand-up fellas. No worries there."

"Good, because if they ever decided to not be very stand-up, then I hate to think what might become of them under the protective ordinances the town is under."

"That's what I need to learn more about. We may have some visitors coming to town, and knowing how this works could help stop some needless bloodshed."

The librarian nodded, taking out her reading glasses as she leaned in over the documents. Seeing this, Jasmin hesitantly took out a pair of glasses herself and slipped them on. She hated the fact that she needed artificial aide in seeing.

Alma smiled. "Those look good on you. Where did you get them?"

"Um, I buy them in bulk at Costco. I'm always losing them, so I try to keep a pair strategically hidden in every room of my house."

"Brilliant idea. But now, back to the articles. From what

I've learned over the years, these were written and agreed upon by the shifters and humans that founded Singing Falls. Are you familiar with the founding of the town?"

"I am. I know that it was the basis for our yearly First Eve Festival. But I didn't know that there was an agreement forged to prevent harm from being done."

"Yes, there was a verbal agreement that was later added to the town charter. As you can imagine, with so many supernatural beings and humans coming together, there came to be considerable tension in the town. The humans feared the supernaturals; some of the supernaturals feared members of their own community. So, an order was given that in order to live in Singing Falls, no violence could be committed by supernaturals or humans."

"And how was this enforced? Was it just a handshake deal? Because I really don't see that holding. It would also explain why there has been a rash of violence lately, of which I'm sure you've heard about."

"There are no records of how the amendment was enforced. But if you look here—" she pointed to the actual amendment that forbid mystical violence, and a line of signatures underneath, "—this was signed by the leaders and founding fathers at the time. And then there is this one signature here, that stands out from the rest. I've never found reference to who this person is."

The signature in question was written in cursive in faded red print, whereas all the other names were in black ink. Crudely printed, and some marked only by an 'X'. The name in red was Ruby Clandon.

Jasmin stared at the name, not daring to blink.

"Does this name mean anything to you?" asked Alma.

Jasmin swallowed hard. "Yes. Clandon is the name of

my ancestors. And Ruby was my great-great-great grandmother."

Alma looked at her with surprise.

"Well, this is hugely important," said Alma.

"What do you mean?"

"Why would a witch sign an agreement on the founding of a town? I have spent countless hours researching this name and come up blank. Is there a reason she would not appear in the town registers from back then?"

"I honestly don't know. But there has to be a reason."

"If a witch of your lineage signed this document, then maybe it wasn't just a verbal agreement after all."

Jasmin thought for a moment, leaning in to read the amendment again. "It says here that the only violence against a supernatural or human to be tolerated was if it were in true defense of one's own life. Aggressive actions for the sake of dominance or feeding would not be tolerated."

"That's why there were no werewolves allowed in Singing Falls. Or vampires for that matter. At least not until your friends moved to town."

Jasmin pondered this in silence before realization struck her.

"Both Max and Elric have not broken this amendment. They have only ever acted out of self-preservation or to protect someone else. Maybe whatever this article is tied to, hasn't been triggered because they haven't broken the law of the land."

"Perhaps you are right. I don't know enough about such things. But it sounds reasonable."

Jasmin turned to Alma, and the librarian could read the question on her face before she asked.

"Alma, I know this is a big ask, but can I take these? I will take very good care of them, but I need to study them with a friend of mine. There may be a way we can figure out more about what this is tied to."

"Of course, dear, but do promise not to let any harm come to them. They are a very important piece of this town's history. I'll get you a special travel box to store them in."

When she disappeared to get the box, Jasmin read over the articles yet again. Why had her ancestors been a part of the signing of something like this? She needed to get this back home where she and Torie could examine it under a different kind of light.

The thought of her friend caused her brow to furrow in worry. The thought of Torie out in the woods, stalking or being stalked by a werewolf caused her anxiety to flare up. But Torie was tough. She could handle herself.

She could only hope that Torie had as much belief in herself as Jasmin did.

"Here you go, dear," said Alma. She placed a gray box lined with velvet and silk on the table. "I'll bundle this up for you. How exciting, you're about to have an adventure, I can tell. You're so lucky! Please promise you'll let me know what you find out."

Jasmin smiled at the librarian. "Alma, would you like to give me your number? Maybe you can swing by the house later to meet my friend. Maybe we'll have an adventure together."

The librarian's eyes grew wide.

"Why, I would love that. If you're serious."

"Of course. And you seem to know more about this town than anyone else I've met, so we may need your help."

Alma blinked her eyes rapidly. "I...I haven't been needed for anything in so long. I don't know what I can do, but yes…I'll help in any way I can." She cleared her throat. "Um, will Fionna be there?"

Jasmin nodded. "Is that a problem?"

"No, not at all. It might be good to see her after so much time."

Jasmin didn't question her as she scribbled down her number on a piece of paper from her purse and handed it to the librarian. Something told her there was more to the older woman than met the eye, and she was determined to find out what that was.

Chapter Six

The ride to the northern ridge on the outskirts of town was made in near silence. Torie had attempted small talk a couple of times, only to receive one-word answers or grunts from Max. He wasn't in the mood to talk, and eventually she gave up, settling back in her car seat and listening to the squawks and coded messages that came across his police frequency radio from time to time as they made their way up the mountainous roadside.

The northern ridge was a scenic part at the uppermost county lines where Singing Falls was located. It was undeveloped and wild, overgrown with dense forestry and boulder outcroppings that made for majestic views for those that were brave enough to hike up to them, and then out onto the slippery rocks to take a peek.

There were hiking trails that had been forged by intrepid explorers since before the founding of the towns, but they were little more than single-file dirt paths that were barely recognizable if you didn't know what you were looking for.

Max eased his car off the road and hopped out, heading for a break in the tree line. Torie filed out after him and hurried to catch up. She hadn't expected him to open the car door for her, but she had thought he would have at least waited on her before heading into the dense undergrowth.

One of the things that Torie loved so much about the town she had recently moved to was the natural beauty that surrounded her. The air was clean and crisp everywhere she went, and there was more greenery than she had ever known in her lifetime. The wooded area they entered was nothing short of breathtaking in its beauty, but she also knew that such wild areas were rife with dangers.

As if he read her mind, Max turned to speak to her as he kept walking. "Be careful and try to step where I step. We are going fairly high up into the ridgeline and there are sudden drop-offs you can't see until it's too late."

Almost immediately, Torie felt the change in terrain as they began their ascent up the mountain. She dug her boots in and felt her thighs start to burn slightly as she followed behind the wolf. She could tell that he was moving at a pace slower than he would have liked for her benefit and part of her wanted to tell him to speed up, while another part was thankful he slowed.

After a half-hour, Torie stopped, gulping lungfuls of air while trying to mentally extinguish the fire in her legs and back.

"You okay?" Max removed a water bottle from his belt and handed it to her.

"Thank you," she said. Why hadn't she thought to bring water?

"You're the one that wanted to come, remember? And I thought you'd be stronger or something. How is this walk winding you?"

Torie huffed and all but threw the water back at him.

"I'm a witch, Max, not bionic. What is your problem with me? I'm not your enemy here. I've been nothing but good to you, and I don't ask you for anything."

"I don't have a problem with you, Torie. And you're right, you don't *ask* for anything." He turned to restart the hike but swung back around when he realized she wasn't following.

Torie stared hard at the werewolf. The inflection of what he had just said wasn't lost on her.

"Are you saying I took something from you? I don't know you well enough to…" She paused, looking at the wolf. "Elric. You think I took Elric from you."

Max rolled his eyes, but the speed with which he looked away from her told her she was on the right path.

"I'm sorry if that's how you feel. I promise you that was not my intention. I didn't plan for any of this. I can only imagine how you must feel."

Max's face grew tight as he walked up to her.

"No, you can't imagine. You can't imagine what it's like because you're not a wolf. You don't know what it's like to have a beta that you have always depended on; someone who has your back no matter what, and then have them suddenly…gone. Then, when they're gone, you realize that you're alone. Truly and completely alone. No pack, no mate, no beta…and then you realize that this is how your existence is going to be; for a very long time." He dropped his head, and Torie thought she could see red rising in his cheeks.

"You're not alone, Max. You still have Elric; maybe not as your beta, and honestly, I'm not really sure I understand what that meant completely, but he's there as your friend. Not because of some wolf edict that he obeys you; but as a friend who wants to do what's best for you. And he isn't the only one. We're your pack now; me, Jasmin, Fionna, Glen... all of us."

The wolf didn't say anything, but Torie could feel he was on the cusp of an emotional outburst and instinctively she reached out and hugged him. His body was stiff at first, before he slowly raised his hands and put them around her, letting his body sink into hers.

"I'm sorry," he said, pulling away. "I shouldn't have said all that. And it's not really how I feel. It's just everything that is happening right now has brought back so many painful memories, and I'm feeling a little overwhelmed. I don't want to face my brother, and it's taken all the strength I have not to run from all of this."

Torie smiled at the big wolf. "Trust me. Running from your problems doesn't solve them; it draws them out, makes them fester until they end up doing even more damage than if you'd dealt with them in the first place."

"You know, for what it's worth, I think you and Elric make a fine couple. A witch and a werewolf. Never would I have ever imagined such a thing. Makes about as much sense as a werewolf and a vampire I guess, so who am I to judge?"

They continued walking, each re-energized after the brief stop.

"Why is it so...I don't know...taboo for shifters to fall in love outside of their race?" asked Torie.

"Shifters fall for other shifters all the time. But they are both still shifters. Vampires are not shifters. Humans are most definitely not shifters. As far as vampires go, there is a history there with werewolves that makes it so that neither of them would ever consider crossing that line."

"Why?"

"Because werewolves were at one time considered slaves of the vampires. We were their daylight guardians. They kept us as pets."

Torie stopped walking, staring at the back of Max's head. "That's terrible."

"It was what it was. Thankfully, we evolved beyond that. Or, more like we rebelled beyond that."

Torie wasn't sure what to say as they moved slowly, continuing up the ridge.

"That would explain your animosity towards vampires. But you're cool with Elion, though, right?"

"He's one of the few good ones. Or at least of the few that I know. Just like wolves, we aren't all bad. We just have bad reputations."

He wheeled to face her; his eyes locked on hers. Then, in a flash, he shifted into his hybrid form and lunged at her with a roar. His enlarged snout opened to reveal dagger-like fangs and extended claws reached for Torie as he sprinted forward almost faster than the eye could follow.

Before she could stop him, he had one massive hand on her arm and shoved her forcibly to the ground. She landed on her back, rolling to the side as shock dimmed her pain response. All the breath was knocked out of her lungs and she struggled to sit up, her head throbbing, vision blurry.

She could make out Max as he wrestled with something. Something large and gray. It was a wolf, and it must have charged out of the undergrowth, coming up behind where Torie had been standing. Locked in a deadly embrace, they snarled at one another. The gray wolf was large, nearly the size of a small pony, and it struggled against Max, pressing its size and weight to gain momentum and pin the hybrid werewolf down.

On his back, Max kept his forearm under the wolf's

throat, preventing the powerful jaws from closing on his own. With his other hand, he formed a fist and drove it into the beast's side, landing two thunderous punches that caused the creature to rear back its head and howl in pain.

Using his own claws, Max sliced at the underside of the wolf, tearing a long, bloody trench into its side. The wolf howled again and leapt back, giving Max time to roll to his feet and charge the wolf. Claws extended, he reached for the werewolf's neck, but before he could make contact, another form came charging out of the tree line and barreled into him, sending him flying to the side to land in a heap just off the trail.

This wolf was reddish-brown and nearly as large as the gray. The two of them advanced slowly on the sheriff, a menacing growl rumbling from their deep chests. Max roared back in defiance, baring his fangs and flexing his claws as he braced for their attack.

The red wolf leapt, but then froze in mid-air, caught in a gleaming blue light that emanated from Torie's outstretched hands.

The witch held the werewolf fast, her lips moving silently as she invoked her hex powers. With a heave, she hurled the creature away from them, sending it crashing into the undergrowth. Her hands glowed with power as she turned to Max.

"You alright?"

His response was a growl. One that her magic interpreted as meaning, "Fine, but pissed".

The red wolf gathered itself and stared at Torie, eyes blazing and fangs dripping saliva. It charged at the witch, covering an incredible amount of ground in only a few bounds. Torie had a shield up before it reached her, and it crashed into her magic with a thud. Rearing up on its hind legs, it flailed at the mystic shield, raking its claws against the barrier and causing sparks to fly in attempts to reach its prey.

Max moved to help but was cut off by the gray wolf as it circled between them, charging at the sheriff with fangs bared.

Max met the attack head on. He grabbed the large beast by the head, holding its mouth open with both hands. Then, slowly, he began to exert pressure in opposite directions, forcing the werewolf's jaws farther and farther apart until a wet, popping sound could be heard, and Torie looked on in horror as he slit the creature's mouth apart, dropping the carcass as he turned to face the red wolf.

He moved over to stand next to Torie as the red wolf looked from him to its fallen comrade and back. Beside the hybrid, Torie stood, eyes burning with power and blue globes of magic encircling her fists.

The wolf lowered its eyes, ears flattened against the back of its head, and it turned, bolting for the woods and disappearing within a matter of seconds.

Max shifted back to his human form as he gulped in air and tried to steady his racing heart. His arms and torso were splattered in blood as he looked at the dead wolf that lay before them.

"Christ," said Torie. "That is a mess. What do we do with it? Should I incinerate the body?"

"No, I'll drag it deeper into the woods and leave it. Let the body return to ground. There are a lot of nutrients in werewolves."

Torie wrinkled her nose at the thought. "Max, since he's dead, shouldn't he return to his human form?"

"Not always," said the sheriff. "It depends on what form they were born in. Some shifters are born in their animal form and learn to shift to human. If that's the case, then this was his natural form, which he will retain in death."

"Well, I'll file that away in things I never thought I'd have to know."

Max turned to her. "Thank you for the save, Torie."

"And thank you as well."

He smiled. "And for what it's worth, your magic is way cooler than anything the *Bionic Woman* could have ever done."

Torie laughed, still trying to catch her breath. "So, what now? Did you know those wolves?"

Max shook his head. "No, but I recognized their scent. They were pack mates from the Idle Winds." He took a deep breath and turned to face her. "They were scouts. We need to get back to town and let Elric and Sable know. The one that got away will let my brother know that I'm here. He will be mounting a full-scale attack soon, and he won't care who he has to hurt to get what he wants."

He didn't have to say it. Torie knew that what his brother wanted was blood. Max's blood as well as Elric's. And she wasn't about to allow that to happen.

Chapter Seven

As they pulled into the driveway at Torie's house, she pulled her face back in from the open window and hurriedly exited the vehicle.

"Honestly, do I smell that bad?" asked Max, closing his door as he climbed out.

"You need a shower. Immediately," Torie replied, holding her nose as she pushed through the front door. Dead werewolf flesh was probably the worst thing she had ever smelled in her life. And that included the time her ex-husband had somehow managed to drop shrimp behind their sofa and they had to bring in a special canine to locate the source of the offending odor weeks later.

Max headed for the door, only to have her block his way.

"Nope, you are not tromping through my house with shifter splatter on you. Go around through the garage, leave your uniform and then go right down the hall to the service room and clean up."

She headed back through the house, checking her cell

phone as she walked. Still no message from Elric. She had texted him as soon as they had service and tried calling as well. Her call went straight to voicemail so either he was somewhere with no reception, or he had his phone off. The latter didn't seem like something he would do, and if he were in town, he'd have reception.

She tried not to think what either of those scenarios could mean as she made her way to her study.

"Leo?" she called out, looking around her favorite room in the house. She found the little dragon curled into a ball on a cushion under her desk. He had the run of the house now, but that was definitely his favorite spot when left alone.

"There you are. Are you ready to eat? Is my little man hungry?"

At the mention of eating, the dragon perked up, his snout high in the air as he stretched his back, vibrating his tail slightly.

"That's a good boy. What a big stretch! Come on, let's get some food."

She held out her hand, and Leo leapt onto it, then made his way quickly up her arm onto her shoulder. Together, they walked back into the kitchen where she took out a platter of raw steak cut into cubes and covered with plastic wrap.

She took a few pieces and placed them in a porcelain serving bowl that sat on the floor near the French doors that led to the deck. Immediately, Leo leapt to the bowl and picked up one of the squares with his little paws and began munching on it.

Torie smiled. She loved watching him eat. For something that would one day grow into a ferocious beast, he had a dainty way of eating that never failed to delight her.

Just then, the front door opened and both Elric and

Sable entered the house, both breathing heavily and laughing. Torie frowned when she saw her boyfriend.

"And where have you been? I called you and texted," she said.

Elric's face knotted up in concern. "I'm sorry. We went for a run. Needed to burn off some stress and energy, so we took to the woods and made our way here. Reception is spotty through there, and I didn't think to check my phone before we got here."

He pulled out his cell and saw the missed messages from Torie.

"Is everything okay? What happened?"

"It's fine now. We were jumped by a couple of Arin's errand boys, but no biggie." It was Max's voice that drifted from the hall behind them.

Everyone turned as the big wolf entered the room, using a towel to dry his shaggy hair as he entered. Torie's eyes grew large and then looked away as she realized the towel he was drying his head with was one he should have had around his waist.

Wolves were not known for their modesty, and other than her, no one else in the room, including Sable, seemed to notice.

"Scouts?" asked Elric. He turned to Torie, his face a mask of concern. "Were you hurt?"

"No, I'm fine. We both are."

"She's more than fine," said Max. "She handled herself, and those wolves, like a pro. I'd probably have been killed had it not been for her."

Torie blushed. Though she wasn't sure if it was his words or the fact that he was now strolling over to the refrigerator, naked and nonchalant.

"Okay, can you at least put on some pants?" she said,

turning to check on Leo and to look out the back door. The dragon had finished his meal and was licking at the sides of the bowl before looking up at Torie in expectation of more, his emerald eyes wide and pleading.

She looked at him and shook her head. Part of her wanted to feed him more; he was the same size now as when he had shown up on her doorstep, and she wondered if maybe she wasn't feeding him enough.

Unfortunately, there were no guidebooks out there on raising a dragon. She had no idea what the normal growth chart was for such a creature. Even Elion had been no help with that, and he knew more about dragons than Torie could have ever imagined.

Elric watched her, reading her concern about the little dragon.

"Did you ever reach out to the vet down in Trinity Cove?"

Torie nodded her head. "I did. Unfortunately, she is out of town and there was no word as to when she would be back."

"What about that new lady who just moved to town? Emma Kyle, if I remember correctly," said Max. "She's a vet. I met her at the courthouse looking into what is needed to open a new business here in town."

"I'm not sure just any veterinarian will be able to help me with Leo," said Torie.

"Something tells me she isn't just any vet," replied Max. "She definitely didn't smell human."

"Okay, can we just talk for a moment about how unseemly it is for you to go around smelling people? It's rude," said Torie.

Max blinked, staring at her. Then he waved a hand in

Elric's direction. "It's not like I do it on purpose. It's second nature. He does it too, you know."

Elric raised both hands, stepping back. "Hey, don't make your problem my problem. And didn't Torie ask you to go put on pants?"

"Yeah, yeah, I'm going," he said. He walked out of the kitchen, throwing a look back at Elric and playfully shaking his head.

"Are you sure you're okay?" asked Elric again.

"For the hundredth time, yes," Torie said, moving to give him a quick, reassuring peck on the lips. She felt her ears burning and knew Sable was watching them, but she couldn't bring herself to turn and face her. She had to remind herself that this was her boyfriend's fated mate, and Torie wasn't sure how seeing him with someone else might affect her.

Sable cleared her throat and spoke up. What she said was not what Torie was expecting to hear.

"Thank you." Her voice was low and raspy, somehow making her even more earthy and appealing.

Torie turned to face her, her eyebrows arched as she pointed towards herself. "Me? Was that for me?"

Sable smiled. "Yes. Thank you for taking such great care of Elric. Thank you for seeing past the wolf to the man beneath." She looked at the big wolf, and Torie could see him blush in response. "What he did was incredibly brave, leaving the safety of his pack, striking out on his own with Max. I'm glad he found someone who made him want to settle down."

Her words piqued Torie's curiosity. This woman knew more about Elric than he had let on.

"Elric," Torie said, "would you mind walking Leo? He usually has to go right after eating."

The wolf looked at the two women and then down at the dragon. Torie could practically see his mind whirling as he tried to come up with an excuse to stay in the kitchen.

"Well…I mean, what if he won't go for me?"

"He will." Torie leveled her gaze at her boyfriend. "Besides, I want to spend some time with Sable. We need to get to know one another a little better."

Elric started to speak up again but knew there was no point. Instead, he just smiled and nodded, bending down to pick up the dragon.

"Oh, why don't you take Max with you as well?" said Sable. Elric glared but nodded as he walked towards the back of the house to get the sheriff. After some mumbled voices that the two women could not make out, they heard the garage door open and close, letting them know they were alone in the large house.

"Good call on sending Max out with him," Torie said.

"Max has ears like…well, a wolf. And anything he overhears he will tell Elric. Those two are inseparable."

"Well, now they are. They went through a rough patch a while back," said Torie.

Sable cocked her head slightly to one side. "But they are alpha and beta. They are two sides of one coin."

"True. But when they first arrived in town, there was definitely friction between them. Things have healed over, but something nearly drove a wedge between them. Still not sure what it was."

Sable smiled, pulling up a chair to the island. "I think you're looking at that wedge."

Torie moved to the counter behind the island and poured herself a cup of coffee. She offered one to Sable as well, but the woman shook her head politely.

"Wait, did Max have a thing for you or something?" asked Torie.

"Not at all. He was upset that Elric was denying the fated mate bond. On one hand he knew that nothing would bring the two packs together after he...wait, how much do you know about what happened?"

"Only what Elric shared. I know that Max's wife was killed and in return, he took the life of his brother's mate."

Sable nodded. "Those were dark times. Still are. Max knew there was no going back from that act. His brother would either kill him or he would have to kill his brother."

Torie sipped her coffee and shook her head slowly.

"It sounds so...warlike. Their existence with the pack."

"I suppose to an outsider it could seem that way. It was all about dominance and control of the territory. My pack, the Idle Winds, held the high ground above the lake. But the game in that area was limited and drying up more and more with each passing season. Max's pack held a smaller, but more fertile, territory. So as with any warring clans, it all came down to our desire to control the better grounds."

"Did it ever occur to them to simply sit down and share the hunting grounds?"

Sable nodded. "Yes, that topic was raised many times by the elders in our pack. but Arin was not one to listen to the council of others. In order to share a hunting ground, the two packs would have to merge into one. And that was fine, except that each pack had an alpha in charge. One of them would have to leave the pack voluntarily, and that is a behavior that is typically not in either one's nature."

"So, the fact that you and Elric, from two different packs, were fated mates. Was that seen as a potential way to bring the packs together?"

"Perhaps. It was unheard of, and the elders for both

packs saw it as an omen that could mean great things for the future. If our union was allowed."

"Arin took it as a sign that he would be ousted from his position as alpha. He believed that me taking the beta of another pack as my lover would give Max's pack too much leverage, too much control. That's when he started the raids on his brother's pack. The raids that eventually led to Max's wife being killed and Max doing what he did for revenge."

She paused, peering out the picture window into the distance. Torie could see how hard it was for her, and she couldn't imagine what the wolf was feeling as she was forced to dredge through such horrible memories.

"But Arin, in his rage, decreed that I was to be his new mate, and that Max and Elric were to be put to death. It was unheard of…to force someone who was fated to another to become your mate. It wasn't what I wanted, and yet I had no one to turn to. No one except for Elric and Max.

"Max offered me asylum in his pack, but that would have meant certain death not only for him but everyone in the pack. So, he did what he felt was best as a leader. He left, taking on the role of lone wolf, and leaving the pack in the hands of their elders, until a new alpha would rise. It was all the Elders could do to keep the pack whole and from falling into all out civil war."

"And I take it Elric did not want the position?"

"No. He was a beta. A follower, not a leader. It was his choice to leave and follow his alpha."

"And what about you?"

Sable swallowed hard, offering a terse smile to the witch.

"I was left to the tender mercies of Arin. I told myself that it would help to keep the peace. Help to take Arin's mind off Max and Elric. And for a time, that worked. But I wasn't Arella, his wife, and he wasn't my fated mate. He grew more and more...angry and withdrawn. Eventually his thoughts returned to Max and, by extension, Elric.

"He became more and more violent, with the majority of it focused on me. One night, after a particularly bad altercation, I decided I wasn't going to take it anymore. I left the pack under cover of darkness and fled. Eventually, without really knowing why, I made my way to Trinity Cove. I hoped the magic there, and the sheer number of shifters and supernatural creatures, would let me blend in.

"I took a job, tried to disappear into the community. And then, I met Elion." At the mention of the vampire's name, her eyes lit up, and Torie saw a smile spread across her beautiful features. "I won't say it was love at first sight... but it was close. The fact that he was a vampire wasn't lost on me, but in Trinity Cove, no one really paid us any attention."

"So why didn't you stay there? Make that your home?" asked Torie.

"Because, as much as I wanted to give him all of my heart, I couldn't. There was another who held a piece of me." She looked down, unable to meet Torie's gaze.

"Elric," Torie said.

Sable nodded. "And that's why I am here now. Asking you to break our bond. I want to be with Elion, but as long as that bond with Elric exists, I can't fully bond with Elion. No matter how badly I might want it."

Just then, the door swung open, and Jasmin hurried into the kitchen. She gestured over her shoulder with a thumb as she approached them.

"Was that Elric and Max around the side of your house trying to coax your dragon to poop? Cause I really need to snap a picture of that to hold over them later on."

She stopped short as she looked at Sable and Torie.

"Jasmin, please tell me you learned something helpful."

"Still not sure about breaking a fated mate bond," said Jasmin. "But I might have a lead on how to prevent Singing Falls from becoming ground zero in a werewolf pack war."

She placed the document box she had been carrying on the island before them and carefully flipped open the lid.

"Torie, I think this is an original binding spell created by my ancestors, hidden in the founding fathers' documents for Singing Falls. We need to cast it, and hopefully, it will transform Singing Falls into the sanctuary city it was meant to be."

Torie looked at the document and then back up at her friend.

"What does it do once cast?" she asked.

Jasmin looked around, taking a deep breath before answering.

"I think it cures werewolves. Turns them human."

Chapter Eight

Sable stood up, slowly pushing herself back from the island as she stared at the witch. Her face, a mask of confusion, started to give away to one of anger.

"What do you mean 'cures werewolves'?" she said.

"Maybe cure isn't the right word," Jasmin said.

"Cure implies that there's something wrong with us," said Sable. "We were born this way. We don't have a disease."

"That isn't what I meant," Jasmin replied. "Torie, help me out here."

Torie looked at her friend, not quite sure how to answer. "Maybe before this goes any further, why don't you tell us exactly what you *do* mean."

Jasmin took a deep breath, glancing from one to the other. "I think we need to study this document a little more to fully understand it. But from what I can tell, these articles of incorporation speak of a way of preventing supernatural violence in the town of Singing Falls."

"Preventing violence by neutering wolves?" said Sable, folding her arms across her chest.

"I don't see that anywhere on here," said Torie. She had dug around in one of the drawers on the island and retrieved a set of reading glasses. They rested low on her nose, and she leaned over the document, careful not to touch it, as she studied the words.

"Not explicitly, no," said Jasmin. "But if you look here —" she pointed to a portion of the document halfway down the page, "—it talks about the boundaries of the town being clearly delineated. And here, it also refers to the Ley lines not being crossed. That implies that someone knew about the magical influx of energies in this town and how they worked."

She looked over at Torie who was nodding, not taking her eyes off the paper. "True, but just because they knew about the existence of magic, doesn't mean they were manipulating it."

"One of my ancestors was the co-author of this document. I can trace my lineage as a witch as far back as seven generations. That means they did indeed know what they were doing."

"But there's a huge difference between knowing magic and making the leap to imposing what you're talking about," said Sable.

"I have to agree," said Torie. "This could be talking about human laws when it comes to violence, and they simply want to apply them to the supernatural community. Who's to say this isn't just talking about a stricter penalty in the eyes of the law?"

"Do you see this part?" Jasmin pointed to a line at the end of the document.

Both Torie and Sable leaned in close, peering over her shoulder. The line in question stood out because of the change in penmanship. It had obviously been written by someone else. It also wasn't in English.

"What is this?" demanded Sable. "It looks like Latin."

"That isn't Latin," said Torie. "I studied Latin in school for three years, and I don't recognize any of this."

"You're right, it isn't Latin. This is written in the old language of the Hex," said Jasmin. "The original language of the witches."

Both Sable and Torie stared hard at the document. Torie swallowed as she began to understand what her friend was implying.

"So, what does it say?" asked Sable.

Jasmin pursed her lips together, wrinkled her brow, and glanced at Torie before she continued.

"And let it be known with this key, that any beast from man who sheds the blood of man shall forever be locked in their natural form, never again to know or touch their dual nature."

Silence settled across the kitchen as Jasmin's words slowly began to sink in.

"It sounds like a decree, not a spell," said Torie. "And what is this key that is mentioned?"

"Now that I'm not sure about. But the fact that it is written in the language of witches, and it's the only part of this document written that way, I'm pretty sure it's a spell," said Jasmin.

"Then why isn't it working?" asked Torie. "There has been so much bloodshed of late, just since I moved to town. Other than the steps that we have taken to ensure justice, there has been no supernatural repercussions that I am aware of."

"I've been thinking about that, and I think this spell was not completed. It wasn't truly cast once the decree was made."

Torie looked at her friend unflinchingly. She wanted Jasmin to admit it openly to Sable.

Sable stepped back from the island and began pacing the floor. "We both know what she is saying. She wants to finish what was started. She wants the two of you to cast this spell, right?" She turned and gave Jasmin a look that dared the witch to deny what she said.

Jasmin didn't hesitate. "Yes, that is exactly what I am thinking."

Voices echoed down the hall, heralding the arrival of the two werewolves and the young dragon that bounded ahead of them into the kitchen, making a beeline for Torie. He sat on his hind legs as he looked up at the witch, his tail wagging happily.

Torie could not help but smile down at her little friend.

"Well, it looks like someone had a productive walk. Who's a good boy? Who's the best dragon? Did Leo go poop?" She bent down, offering her hand for him to scamper up on.

"Oh, it was productive, alright," said Max, his brow furrowed. "I don't know how so much can come from such a tiny body."

Elric looked around the room at the faces and could tell something was amiss.

"What's going on in here?" he asked.

Max picked up on it as well, turning to the women in concern. "Yeah, what's wrong? Who died?" His statement wasn't hyperbole; in a town like Singing Falls, he was being deadly serious.

"Who died? No one yet, but it will be us if this witch has

her way," said Sable, as she leveled Jasmin with a steely gaze.

"What are you talking about?" demanded Elric, turning his attention to Torie and Jasmin.

"Jasmin found something at the library," said Torie. "It's an original copy of the founding articles when the town was incorporated. There's a clause in it that was written in the language of the Hex. She thinks it's a spell that was set in order to prevent supernaturals from killing humans."

Max and Elric were silent, knowing there had to be more to the story than that.

"And?" said Max.

"And tell them how the spell would work," said Sable.

Jasmin cleared her throat. "If I understand it correctly, it will turn a shifter who commits violence into a human. I am assuming that would make it easier for them to then be subjected to the laws of man."

She read to them the passage word for word.

Max shook his head. "This can't be what it means. It says return them to their natural state. But shifters were born, not created by magic. Our natural form is to be fluid between animal and human."

Jasmin didn't say anything as she stood there chewing on her bottom lip while she stared at the document with everyone else.

"For all I know I've got this all wrong," she said. "Maybe that isn't what this means."

Sable was visibly upset as she watched Jasmin contemplate the paper before them.

"I think you've already made up your mind about this. I think even if you got it wrong, you're hoping you're right, and you witches will find a way to make it so." She turned to face Elric, her eyes blazing. "And you said this was someone I could trust to help us. I think I'd rather take my chances with Arin."

With that she shifted to her wolf form and bounded out the back door. Elric called after her, following her to the patio door. He reached it just in time to see her leaping over the iron fence and down onto the grounds below. Before he could say anything else she was racing for the tree line, disappearing in the old growth of the woods that surrounded Torie's house.

"Great. What was all that about, Jasmin?" he said.

"It was about doing what we need to do to protect this town."

"You should have just told her that it wasn't an option," Elric said.

Jasmin didn't say anything, only glancing at Torie who found herself unable to meet her friend's gaze. She walked slowly to the other side of the island resting both hands on it as she worded her next sentence very carefully.

"Jasmin, I have to say, I don't think this is a good play."

"You're the one who asked me to help you with this. You said you wanted to break the bond between them in order to prevent a bloody showdown in this town."

"Yes, you're right. But I didn't think the only way to do it would be to rob them of who they truly are."

Jasmin visibly flinched; her friend's words had hurt her.

"I don't think you understand how a fated mate bond works," said Jasmin. "You can't just sever something like that. I don't know how casting this spell will impact their bond, but it will make Singing Falls into the sanctuary it was always meant to be."

"But that peace would come at a terrible price," said Max. The big sheriff had been unusually quiet throughout the conversation. "You say this will revert shifters back to their natural form. But you do know there are shifters that were born in their animal form and then learn to shift to a human, don't you?"

"He's right," said Elric. "What about those? Are you saying that this spell, once cast, will revert them back to an animal form? For good?"

"Only if they do something that violates the laws that the spell will abide by," said Jasmin. "You know as well as I do that pretty much everybody in this town has never so much as jaywalked, let alone shed the blood of another. They're not going to be impacted by this in the least."

Elric didn't say anything as he moved to stand by Max. His arms were folded and his eyes were pleading with Torie, begging her to intervene.

"How would this impact Max? He's law enforcement, so there's going to be times where he may have to do what's necessary to protect the community," said Torie. "I mean, he saved my life today. What if this spell were in effect when that happened?"

Jasmin didn't respond, and Torie could tell the question was swirling in her mind. But she also knew her friend. And part of her was afraid that Jasmin had already made up her mind.

"Can this spell be reversed?" asked Torie.

"Why would we reverse it?" Jasmin screwed up her nose. "But I suppose, like any spell, once cast it can be recalled."

"I'm just thinking that if we put this in place just while we deal with Max's brother, it could give us a chance to sit down and talk with them and let cooler heads prevail. If they know there are consequences to attacking anyone in the town, and that includes Max, Elric, and Sable, it might make them think twice."

No one said anything as Max stalked over to the large picture window, his gaze focused on the outside. He turned to face the women as an idea struck him.

"If this spell was such a good idea in the first place, why wasn't it cast?" he asked.

"Good question," said Elric. "Maybe it's because your ancestor knew this was not a good idea."

"I don't know why it wasn't cast. Who knows, maybe it was, and it didn't work."

Torie could feel the tension building in the air. She wanted nothing more than to defuse the situation and calm everyone down before someone said something that couldn't be taken back.

"Why don't we all just take a breather and think about this. I know I could use a break to clear my head, and I'm sure the two of you could as well." She looked at Elric and Max, hoping they would get the hint and stand down.

"You're right," said Jasmin. "Maybe we need to just take a breather. I promise you I'm coming from a good place with this. But I'm also not going to act alone. If this is something you are firmly against, then maybe we can find another way."

Torie smiled, deep down she knew her friend would be open to reason.

Before they could respond, the front door to Torie's home burst open, and Fionna came running into the space.

"You guys! Why haven't you answered your phones?" she said, nearly out of breath.

Torie spun to face her as she dug into her pocket and hauled out her cell phone.

"It's on silent, I didn't even realize it had gone off. We were kind of in the middle of a pretty heavy discussion. What's going on?"

"There's been a murder in town. Max, I think you need to get over there as soon as possible."

"On my way," said the wolf as he headed for the back of the house to gather his things. "Where did it happen?"

"At the bed and breakfast. The one Sable is staying at."

Chapter Nine

In a flash Elric had shifted into his wolf form and bolted out the back door, taking the same route as Sable into the woods.

Max had thrown on his police vest and boots and raced through the garage to his squad car. Tires squealed and gravel was thrown everywhere as he peeled out onto the road, his siren fading in the distance as he headed for town.

Jasmin grabbed her keys and headed for the front door. "Come on, we need to get there before word of this spreads." As they fastened in, she turned to face Fiona. "How did you hear about this?"

"I was at the bakery looking at the floor plans and thinking about the easiest way to move the display cases to the back of the shop. You know, if we did that then I believe customers would be more focused on—"

"Fionna, just get to the murder," Jasmin said, her voice a little terser than she meant.

"Oh yeah, I was at the bakery, and I heard shouting coming from up the street, you know the bed and breakfast is just around the corner, so I stepped out and could see the commotion and someone was yelling something like 'Oh my God she's dead, she's dead'. I went up the sidewalk and found one of the staff members standing there in shock. When I asked her what happened, she said it was terrible, that someone had just found a body."

"Do you know who it was?" asked Torie.

Fionna shook her head. "No, as soon as I heard about it, I hightailed it over here after you guys didn't answer the phone."

"Are you okay?" Torie asked.

The squirrel shifter was still trying to catch her breath, and Torie noticed just how disheveled she looked.

"Fionna, how did you get here? Where is your car?" asked Jasmin, glancing at her friend in the rear-view mirror.

"It's at the bakery. Would have taken too long to drive here, so I shifted and ran through the woods. Um, Torie... did you mean to bring your little friend?"

"What? Oh, goodness. I forgot he was sitting there." Leo was still perched on Torie's shoulder, half hidden behind her hair.

"What in the...?" said Jasmin, glancing sideways at her friend. "We can't take a dragon to an active crime scene. What if someone sees him?"

Torie reached up and scratched the dragon's belly. "Oh, he won't cause any problems. Besides, he still appears as a cat to humans. Plus, I can leave him in the car if it makes you feel better. I just feel bad that I haven't gotten to spend much time with him today. He gets lonely locked away in the house by himself."

"Maybe you should get a dog or something," said Fionna. "He might like a baby brother or sister."

"He might eat it," mumbled Jasmin, just loud enough to illicit a menacing look from Torie.

"So, what were you two talking about with Max and Elric? It must have been really important that none of you picked up your phones."

Torie and Jasmin exchanged looks, but neither hurried to answer her question.

"Fine," Fionna said. "Keep your little witchy secrets to yourself." She huffed as she dropped back, sinking into the car seat.

"You know," said Torie, "we should tell her. Let her weigh in on the topic as well."

Jasmin frowned, but only shrugged her shoulders as Fionna excitedly leaned forward, all ears, as Torie turned in her seat to face her.

"Jasmin found an old document that detailed the founding of Singing Falls. In it, it references the town achieving sanctuary status. It would mean that shifters, in particular werewolves, would not be able to visit harm on an innocent. But there would be a catch; there is a spell that we need to cast in order to enforce this law. The spell would make it so that if a shifter harms an innocent human, then that shifter would be locked in their natural form, forever."

Fionna frowned, absorbing what Torie had just said.

"So, they would be stuck in their animal form?" asked Fionna.

"More likely they would be stuck in their human form," replied Torie.

"Oh well that is an easy one then," said Fionna. "I would have to say no to that."

Even though they knew where Fionna would land on the matter, both Torie and Jasmin were a little shocked at her words.

"But it would bring stability to the town," said Jasmin.

"The town is already stable. Yes, there have been some issues lately, but we both know that for the most part those were one-offs, and we were able to handle them," said Fionna.

"But this would be a more permanent solution," said Jasmin. "We would not have to worry about attacks happening in the town. Everyone would be safe."

"I think everyone feels safe already," said Fionna. "You're not a shifter, you don't know what this would mean."

Her words intrigued Torie, and she looked questioningly at her friend. "You're right, Fionna, we aren't shifters. What would doing this mean to the community?"

Fionna considered the question and thought carefully before answering. "It would be worse than being locked away. It would be a type of jail that you can't imagine. Shifters are used to the natural flow of energy that comes when we move from one form to the other. To be cut off from that would be worse than losing a limb."

Torie looked over at Jasmin and could see she had an iron grip on the steering wheel. The muscles in her jaw flexed and relaxed repeatedly as she clenched her teeth together.

No one said anything for the rest of the short trip before they arrived at the bed and breakfast.

Jasmin eased her car to a stop half a block away from where the town police department had set up a roadblock. There was a crowd amassing on the sidewalks to either side of the Victorian-style blue and gray shingle building that had been transformed into the town's premier bed and breakfast.

Getting out of the car, the three friends made their way

down the street, pushing through the townsfolk to get to the officer standing at the steps to the entrance of the bed and breakfast.

"I'm sorry, ladies, but no one is allowed beyond this point," he said, holding up one hand.

"It's okay, we're here with Max," said Torie. She attempted to move forward only to be restrained by his hand on her shoulder.

"Ma'am, I said no one beyond this point."

Before Torie could take any action, Jasmin stepped forward. "We are friends and we're here to help." She waved a hand in front of the officer's face, and his features went slack.

"Of course you are," he said. He stepped aside, ushering the ladies forward.

They walked up the stairs to the porch and made their way inside. There were two police officers consoling a near-hysterical woman sitting at the front desk. To the left was a staircase that led up to where they could hear a lot of voices, including Max's as he gave orders to his officers.

There were a lot of bodies milling about upstairs. The dark blue windbreakers with yellow lettering across the back told Torie, Fionna, and Jasmin they were either with the Crime Scene Investigation unit or with the Singing Falls Police Department. Neither group seemed to pay them any attention. As far as they were concerned, anyone that made it past the perimeter outside and downstairs, and actually got up close and personal to the crime scene must belong there.

They made their way past a couple of technicians conferring in the hall as they followed the sound of Max's voice to one of the guest rooms at the back of the bed and breakfast. The sheriff was walking out just as they approached.

He frowned and looked over their shoulders at the stairway. "How did you get up here? You shouldn't be here."

"We have our ways," said Jasmin, smiling coyly. "What have you found?"

Max looked around uneasily. It was clear he wanted to say something but was afraid there were too many ears around for the conversation they needed to have.

"I heard one of the ladies downstairs say it was an animal attack," said Fionna. "Is that true? What kind of animal attacked someone inside a house? On the second floor no less."

"Ugh, I'd give anything for hearing half as sharp as yours," said Jasmin. She motioned towards the room Max had just walked out of. "Is that where it happened? Is the body still in there?"

"Yes," replied the sheriff, "but it's really not a good time. Our usual medical examiner is out on leave, and this replacement one...well, let's just say he doesn't understand our community." He leveled the three women with a look that conveyed far more than his words.

Jasmin took the big werewolf by his arm and pulled him back into the room. Fionna and Torie followed quickly behind. With a wave of her arm and a whispered incantation, Torie sealed the room against prying ears.

The current M.E was hunched over, examining a body that lay face down on the floor. He had his back to them, and when he turned, he was more than a little shocked by their presence.

"Sheriff, who is this?" he asked. He was an older man, probably in his late sixties, Torie would have guessed. His hair was gray and slicked back in a way that made her think either he was trying to hide a bald spot, or he had worn it that way in his youth and never changed the style. He lifted his wire-rimmed glasses off his nose and peered at her and her friends.

"Uh, Dr. Benton these are some...associates of mine. They help out from time to time on cases when my department is stretched thin. This here is Torie, Jasmin, and Fionna. Ladies, this is Dr. Benton. He's covering while Dr. Fox is out on leave for a bit."

Dr. Benton nodded at the three women, shuffled his clipboard from his right hand to his left so he could shake hands with each of the women in turn.

"Ladies, nice to meet you," he said.

"Likewise, Doctor," replied Torie. "So, what have you found?"

The doctor cast a sideways glance at Max, who simply nodded at the man, encouraging him to share whatever he had found.

"Well, first, this is unlike anything I've ever come across before...and that includes my time spent working as an M.E. up in New York. This woman was killed by an animal of some kind; but it's not like any animal attack I've ever seen."

"How so?" asked Jasmin, glancing down at the body. It was covered by a black cloth; only the back of the woman's head was visible. Her hair was stained red to the point that Jasmin couldn't have guessed what color it should have been.

"Well, first of all, the depth of the slash marks are too big and deep. I mean, maybe if we were in Africa a lion could do this. But there is nothing in North America capable of this. Maybe a bear. But...there is no way a grizzly could have gotten into town and up these stairs without being seen. Plus, I'm not even sure grizzlies are native to this part of the country. I think we need to call in a zoologist."

Max looked at his friends before taking in a deep breath and blowing out. "No, I don't think we will need to do that. What else can you tell us? Was there any ID on the body?"

"No, nothing that we could find." He reached for the cloth covering the body then paused. "Uh, not sure you little ladies want to see this."

When they didn't flinch, he pulled back the covering.

The woman's back was indeed slashed deeply. Claw strikes had cut through skin, sinew and muscle, exposing bone.

"There's also what appears to be bite marks on her legs. Whatever did this was very strong. She was picked up by her leg and tossed a couple of times. And again, I'm no expert on animals, but judging from the puncture wounds I'd say the fangs on this thing were at least four inches long. I don't know any animal in these parts with fangs like that."

"I do…" mumbled Fionna, turning away from the body.

"Also, other than her throat being nearly torn out, the front of her wasn't really savaged. It's almost like the animal most likely inflicted the death bite, then flipped her over and did all this. Why? Rabies maybe…"

As much as the thought disgusted Torie, she had to ask. "Did either of you recognize her?"

"No," said Max. "I'm sure we'll be able to figure out who she is. A town this small, someone will know her."

"Can you turn her over?" asked Jasmin. "I've been around town far longer than either of you. Maybe it's a local. Although, I don't see why a local would be staying in a bed and breakfast."

Again, the medical examiner looked to Max for the okay before moving to gently roll the victim onto her tattered back.

Jasmin gasped, a hand flying to her mouth.

"What? Do you know her?" asked Max.

She nodded. Swallowing hard to find her voice. "That's Alma Condos. The librarian I met with earlier."

At the mention of the woman's name, Fionna turned back around and pushed between her friends to stare at the body. She shrieked, both hands flying up to cover her eyes as she turned to bury her face in Torie's shoulders.

Just then, a deputy walked into the room, giving the women a surprised look.

"I thought you shielded the room?" said Jasmin, whispering to Torie.

"No, just soundproofed. How would it look if someone tried walking in and bumped into an invisible barrier?"

Jasmin nodded in agreement as they turned to see what the deputy wanted. Torie had taken Fionna in her arms and was trying to console the now-crying woman.

"Deputy," said Max. "Did you get the name of who this room is registered to?"

"Yes, sir, I did. It's registered to a woman named Sable Callings."

Max exchanged looks with Torie and Jasmin.

"Call Elric," he said to Torie. "Tell him not to come back into town." He turned to his deputy and gave him a knowing nod. "Get everyone out of here and close down this scene. Round up some of the other men that are...in the know. Tell them to start a sweep of the town. There are rogue wolves around, and I want them found."

The deputy nodded and left the room.

"What are you talking about?" asked the medical examiner. "You think a wolf did this? There are no wolves in this part of North Carolina."

"There are now," said Max as he turned to face the women. "This is my fault. I should not have let that other scout get away. Because of that, this woman is dead. My brother is sending me a message of some kind. Well, message received. I'm not hiding or running anymore. It's time to end this, one way or another."

Chapter Ten

Back in Jasmin's car, Fionna sat silently in the back seat. She held Leo on her lap and slowly stroked the dragon's wings. He curled into a tiny ball, a soft, low purr coming from him.

Torie stood on the sidewalk with Jasmin, watching their friend.

"Jasmin, what is going on? Fionna obviously knows this woman you met with, but she hasn't said anything."

Jasmin nodded. "Alma admitted she knew Fionna when I was speaking with her at the library, but she didn't say how. Come on, let's head over to Jim's and see if she wants to talk about it."

Normally, they would have walked the couple of blocks to the bakery, but Fionna didn't look like she was up to that. Plus, Torie didn't want to leave Leo in the car again, and they still weren't sure how some of the more supernatural members of the community might react if they could see him for what he was.

No one spoke as Jasmin drove the couple of blocks to

their favorite coffee shop and eased into the parking lot. Inside, there were quite a few people enjoying the fresh baked pastries as they sat around in small groups talking quietly. More than once, Torie overheard whispered tones referring to some "horrific attack" or similar verbiage. Word travelled quickly in small towns.

They made their way to their favorite spot opposite the large fireplace and sat down. Leo had been riding on Torie's shoulder, and she reached up and sat him down on the floor at her feet, giving him a mental command not to stray. He huffed before lying down, folding his little wings in and resting his head on her feet.

Fionna sat next to Torie, her eyes focused on something far away. It wasn't until Jasmin gently placed a hand on her shoulder that she realized her friend had been offering her a cup of coffee.

"Thank you, Jasmin," she said, feebly, taking the coffee and placing it on the table before her.

Torie took the cup Jasmin offered her as they all settled back into the high-backed leather chairs.

"Fionna, babe…what's going on?" asked Jasmin. "You can tell us anything. You know that, right?"

At first, the squirrel shifter didn't speak, then, she slowly looked up, tears rolling down her cheeks as she focused on her friends.

"Oh, Fionna," said Torie, reaching over to squeeze her friend's hand. "What is going on? You knew that woman, didn't you?" She fished in her purse and removed a clean tissue and offered it.

"Thank you," said Fionna as she dabbed at her eyes. "I'm sorry. I don't usually fall apart like this."

It was hardly what Torie would have considered falling

apart. She had seen women have total meltdowns over being told their hairdresser was overbooked and they would have to wait to get an appointment. Those days seemed so far away in her memory now.

It was from a different lifetime.

But here, seeing her friend in so much pain and trying valiantly to hide it…her heart ached in empathy, and she wanted nothing more than to make Fionna feel better.

"Fionna, what do you need from us? What can we do?" Torie said.

"You're doing it. Just being here and being willing to listen means the world to me."

"Do you need us to call Glen?" asked Jasmin.

"No. No, she is working, and I don't want to bother her."

Torie looked at her and could sense she wanted to talk about something. It was the same feeling she got when Shawn would call her out of the blue and say he didn't want anything but would let long pauses weigh in during the conversation. There was only one way to move this along; she would have to take control of the conversation.

"Fionna, who was that woman to you? It's pretty obvious you knew her," she said.

Fionna sighed and drew in a long breath. "Alma is…or rather *was*…my ex. We were together before I met Glen."

Torie arched an eyebrow but didn't say anything. She looked over at Jasmin who was listening intently to the discussion.

"I met her when I was much younger. I had just arrived in town and decided I wanted to make Singing Falls my home. And by just arrived, I mean I had left the wooded area outside of town where a lot of us smaller woodland shifters were born and raised. Alma was part of the reason I decided to move into town."

Torie patted her friend's hand. "I'm sorry for your loss. This can't be easy on you."

"Hold up," said Jasmin. "You must have been a child when you met that woman. That sounds sketchy to me."

"Jasmin!"

"Well, it does! That woman is way too old to have been involved with Fionna."

Torie opened her mouth to say something but was stopped by Fionna, who raised her hand.

"No, it wasn't like that. You may not realize it, but shifters don't age the way humans do. Our lifespan is considerably longer. When I met Alma, she was a young woman. And so was I."

Now it was Torie's turn to frown. "Are you saying you're the same age as Alma? I mean, I know you've never celebrated your birthday until recently, but...I never imagined you were..."

"Old?" said Fionna, finishing her friend's sentence. "I don't feel it, but in terms of you humans progression of time, yes, I am old."

Torie sank back in her seat, her mind swimming.

"Why did you break up?" asked Jasmin. "Looks to me like there were still strong feelings there."

"Because she felt bad about what was happening between us as far as the aging thing goes. She was getting older; I wasn't. She felt like it was not fair that I should have to waste my years taking care of her as she aged. She felt like she was robbing me somehow. I told her it was nonsense, but over the years, she saw it. Eventually, she made the decision that we were to go our separate ways."

"Can I ask, how long were you together?" said Torie.

"About twenty years I believe."

Jasmin and Torie gasped in unison.

"And how long ago did you break up?" asked Jasmin.

"Oh...I guess that happened maybe thirty plus years ago," said Fionna as she sipped from her cup.

Both of her friends said nothing as they sat there staring at the shifter.

"So, when you told us you don't really know how old you are, or when your birthday was...you were being serious," said Torie.

"Oh absolutely. Like I said, it's not something we celebrate in the shifter world. We don't measure the passing of our own time like that."

Torie's face darkened and before she could stop herself, she blurted something out. "Do all shifters have longer life spans than humans?"

Jasmin glanced at her friend, already knowing where she was headed with her line of questioning.

"I can't speak for all shifters of course, but I would say yes," said Fionna. "I mean, we aren't as long lived as vampires, of course. They don't age and die. As long as they aren't killed, they just keep going. But shifters do get older and eventually we all die of old age. Just like humans."

Torie looked at Jasmin. "Did you know about this?"

Jasmin shook her head. "Fionna is the only real shifter I've ever been friends with. It's not something that has ever come up in conversation between us."

Torie was obviously flustered but didn't say any more. She reminded herself that this was about Fionna and helping her work through her pain; it wasn't about Torie Bliss and what she was feeling.

"Look, I've brought everyone down with my nonsense," said Fionna. "I should probably just go." She moved to stand, only to have Torie grab her hand and motion for her to remain seated.

"Don't be ridiculous. You've suffered a loss, and you shouldn't be alone right now."

"Torie's right," said Jasmin. "We don't have to talk about this anymore, unless you want to. There is a lot happening right now that we need to figure out next steps for."

"Agreed," said Torie, taking out her cell phone. "Elric still hasn't gotten back to me. I hope everything is okay."

"He went after Sable. If Max was right, and his brother is somewhere in the area, then she might be in danger. And so is Elric, and by extension, you, Torie."

"I can take care of myself and so can Elric. Besides, if he were in any real danger, I'd sense it through the connection we share."

Jasmin nodded. "So where do we go from here?"

Fionna's body stiffened as she looked up at her friends.

"Cast the spell," she said, her voice as steely as her gaze. "That's where we go. The two of you figure out how to cast that spell."

Neither of the witches said anything; they just stared at Fionna.

"Fionna, after what you've just seen...maybe you shouldn't be making any decisions like that," said Torie.

"No. It's because of what I just saw that I can make that decision. I was wrong earlier. Alma would still be alive if it weren't for werewolves." She looked at Torie, her eyes wet as she held back tears. "I'm sorry, Torie...I don't mean anything personal by this, but werewolves are monsters. What they did to Alma is who they really are. Max and

Elric aside, there are reasons they have the reputations they do."

She turned away, wiping at her eyes as she took a deep breath and exhaled slowly.

"There is a reason they were never allowed here in Singing Falls. And now, not only do we have two of them living here, but we've accepted a vampire into our midst as well. Jasmin was right; we need something to protect the peaceful citizens of this town."

Torie swallowed hard, her heart racing. She understood where her friend was coming from, but she also knew that what they were considering could drive a wedge between her and her boyfriend.

There it was again. She berated herself at the thought. When had she become so selfish in what she wanted? Her friend was in pain, and all she could think about was how it impacted her.

"Maybe it shouldn't be us that makes this decision," said Torie, her brow furrowed in thought. "Or rather, maybe it shouldn't be just us."

"What do you mean?" asked Jasmin.

"Well, we have taken it upon ourselves to do what is best for this town as we see it. But we don't live here alone. Why don't we ask the community what they think?"

Fionna and Jasmin stared at her, not quite sure if what she was asking was possible.

"How would we do that?" asked Fionna. "Especially given that the town is so mixed."

"Well, since this would primarily affect the shifter population, we could convene a town hall of sorts, just for the supernaturals, and put it to a vote."

Jasmin frowned. "I don't know about that. It could just start a panic by putting it out there."

"I think it's a good idea. I mean, no offense, but neither of you are shifters…and you're going to do something that will have a lasting impact on all shifters," said Fionna.

"You were just all for it a minute ago," said Jasmin.

"And I still am. But I have my reasons. I also don't want to speak for everyone else."

"C'mon, Jasmin," said Torie. "It will make things easier for all of us if we know we have the backing of the community. Isn't that what Singing Falls is built on; community?"

"And if the vote goes in favor of casting the spell, you'll be all in?" Jasmin asked, directing her attention to Torie.

"One hundred percent," she said.

"Fine. I'll speak with some of the business owners, see if we can't find a space large enough. Fionna, can you spread the word? Discreetly…we don't want the humans finding out and showing up out of curiosity."

Fionna nodded and rose to her feet. "I'll let you know what they say. When are we looking to do this?"

"The sooner the better," said Jasmin. "Alma was killed by a werewolf. We can't wait around for Max's brother to send us another message."

Torie reached down and picked up Leo. "C'mon baby, let's get you home and feed you."

At the mention of food, the dragon perked up, his snout quivering in anticipation.

Just as they headed out the door, Torie's cell phone rang. The front lit up with Elric's name, and she found herself smiling as she held the phone to her ear.

"What? Wait, hold on. I'm with Jasmin and Fionna now. Let me put you on speaker phone."

She laid the phone on the coffee table and pressed the speaker button. "Okay, we're all here."

Elric's voice was clearly agitated, and he was out of

breath. "I'm at the police station. I need you to get down here quickly."

"What are you doing at the police station?" Torie asked.

"Max just arrested Sable. He's holding her on suspicion of murdering whoever it was they found at the bed and breakfast this morning."

Chapter Eleven

By the time the three of them had driven across town to the police station, a small mob had gathered outside the building.

"What in the world?" said Torie, as they climbed out.

"There were a lot of witnesses to what happened. People have been talking," said Jasmin. "Also, everyone assembled here seems to be a shifter. Interesting."

They made their way through the crowd that was calling for someone to come out and address them. The anger in the air was palpable as they finally made it to the doors of the building only to find them blocked by two deputies.

"Terrance, Billy," said Jasmin, addressing the officers. "We need to see Max. Now."

The two deputies looked at one another, unsure of what to do.

"Guys, come on," said Fionna. "I've known the two of you since you were just fledglings. We are all in this together, okay. Trust me when I say we are here to help before this situation gets out of control."

The two officers thought over what she said, and the one Jasmin had addressed as Billy nodded his head and whispered something to Terrance.

"Fine. But if Max fires us you have to say you forced us; say that the two witches did some kind of witch mind trick on us."

Jasmin rolled her eyes and pushed past them into the coolness of the police station. Torie could feel the unease in the atmosphere as they made their way towards the reception area.

"We need to see Max," Torie said.

"If you could just have a seat, I'll see if he is available," replied the young man standing behind the desk.

Jasmin huffed. Torie could tell she was getting annoyed with everyone and all the micro delays they were facing.

"Hey, Max," she called loudly, not bothering to look at the officer standing before her. "Let us in, we need to talk."

Max appeared behind the door to the left of the desk and pushed it open for the women. He nodded, letting his officer know it was okay, and stood to the side as they walked past him.

"Max, what is going on out there?" asked Torie.

"And what is going on in here?" demanded Jasmin. "Elric said you arrested Sable and are holding her here? Why?"

The big sheriff led them into his office and closed the door.

"Word has gotten out that the town librarian was killed by a shifter. The townsfolk are not happy because they want to know details," he said.

"Understandable," replied Torie. "And what does that have to do with Sable?"

"Did she do it?" asked Fionna, her voice strained.

"She couldn't have," said Jasmin. "She was with us this morning, and Elric was with her before that."

"The body was found in her room. The only two scents in the room belonged to the librarian and Sable. We have a witness that says she heard two women arguing in that room last evening," said Max.

"Okay, well that doesn't prove she killed anyone. Again, Elric was with her," said Torie.

"The witness also said that she saw Sable with a man... a man that matches Elric's description, but they were only in the downstairs parlor, talking for quite a while. Elric was never seen going upstairs to her room."

"If she did kill her, he would not have seen the body," said Fionna.

"Where is Elric?" questioned Torie.

"He's in back giving a statement to one of the detectives."

Jasmin gave Max a hard look. "Do you really think she did this?"

Max sighed. "No. I don't. But right now, we don't have anything else."

"Then why are you doing this?"

The big wolf returned her hard stare, his hand clenching to a fist as he leaned on the desk.

"Because this is my message to Arin. He wants me dead, but he also wants her. This will bring him to me."

Torie gave him a dismayed look that turned to anger.

"You're using her as bait! I can't believe this."

Max held up both hands. "Now just hold on. In the eyes of the law there is probable cause. Plus, she is safer in here than out there on the streets. That librarian was killed in her room. Arin was showing that he can get to her whenever he wants."

"What does Elric think about this?" asked Torie.

"He thinks this is ridiculous and that Max needs his head examined."

They turned to see Elric walk into the office. He was clearly agitated, and his eyes flashed yellow at Max.

"You know this is the right thing to do," said Max. "We need to end this as soon as possible; that means confronting Arin on our terms."

Torie rolled her eyes and stepped forward between the two wolves. "Or maybe, you could try talking to the man. Is that what you mean by confrontation? Because when I hear you say 'confrontation' I get the impression there won't be a lot of talking."

The two wolves turned their attention to her, and Torie was surprised to see the glare in Elric's eyes as he looked from her to Max.

"That is a good thought, Torie, and in an ideal world that might work. But, and don't take this the wrong way, you don't know the world we live in. Our confrontations are considerably more...active. Less talking."

Torie looked at Elric, not quite sure what to make of his statement. And that's exactly what it was. A statement. No room for discussion or questions. She wasn't used to this kind of attitude from him. She was used to a discourse with the wolf, but something in his tone and demeanor was changing.

"We are having a meeting tonight. With all the shifters in town to discuss this," said Torie. She nodded at Fionna. "As a matter of fact, Fionna, it might be a good time for you to go and speak with the crowd gathering outside. Spread the word that we will meet tonight. We can have it at my house. There is plenty of room, and I'll even provide drinks and light snacks."

Fionna nodded and headed out the door, closing it behind her.

"Torie, I appreciate what you're doing," said Max, "but whatever the discussion is going to be about tonight, it does not involve the town. This is between wolves, and it will be settled between wolves."

Torie looked at Elric, hoping he would step in and calm their friend. No such luck. He stood firm, crossing his arms and nodding in agreement with his old alpha.

"Max don't be so hardheaded. Yes, you can settle this like wolves, but what about the people in the community that get caught in the crossfire? What then?" asked Torie. She could feel the red flush creeping up her neck. "And can we go back to Sable for a moment? What do you think Elion is going to say when he shows up tonight and finds you've locked her in a cage?"

No one spoke, and she was happy to see that her words caused the two men to cast a questioning look at one another.

"What? You didn't think that far ahead?" she said.

Max huffed and drew himself up to his full height.

"This is a police matter, and Elion knows not to interfere in local legal matters. He will have to understand."

Jasmin laughed. "Yeah, I'm with Torie on this one. Where is Elion? Obviously, he isn't around because, one, it's daylight outside, and two, if he were, you would never have arrested Sable. No way he's going to stay on the sidelines."

"And that's a good thing," said Torie. "If it comes down to it, you know we are all on your side. But that's if it comes down to a fight."

Elric was nodding his head in agreement as he turned to address Max.

"She's right," he said. Torie smiled, thankful that her words had finally broken through to him. "We need Elion on our side. He will add considerable muscle; he's more than a match for even their strongest wolves. With him, we can end this in a single night."

Torie's smile turned to a frown. "That isn't what I meant."

But it was too late. Elric had already put the idea out there and Max was nodding in agreement.

"Good idea," the sheriff said. "Can you find him as soon as he shows up tonight and let him know what's going on? In the meantime, I'm going to make sure word gets out that I'm holding Sable. I'm willing to bet Arin won't be able to resist moving on us as early as tonight."

Elric agreed and turned to leave the room. He stopped, swiveling around to face Torie, who simply stared at him. He started to say something, but stopped, opting to nod in her direction and give her an uneasy smile before continuing out the door.

Max picked up his sheriff's hat off the desk and placed it on his head, tipping it at the ladies as he headed for the door as well.

"If you'll excuse me, I have a statement to give to the press."

He left the room without bothering to close the door behind him.

"What...what just happened?" asked Torie.

"Men. That's what happened," replied Jasmin. "They believe in acting first and asking questions later."

"Jasmin, this could get really ugly. What are we going to do?"

"I feel like this is where I should mention we have the answer to that, but you aren't quite ready to pull that trigger."

Torie didn't answer as she glared at her friend.

"Let's go speak to Sable. We need to make sure she's okay and understands what is going on," said Torie.

She led the way out of the office and to the holding cells in the back of the police station. There were only two cells in the small station, and Sable sat quietly in the first one they approached.

"Sable," said Torie, "I am so sorry they are doing this. We're talking with Max about getting you out of here. We know you didn't have anything to do with this."

For someone who had been wrongly arrested and accused of murder, Sable was unusually calm.

"I know. I heard your conversation in there with Max and Elric."

"You heard that?"

The wolf nodded and pointed to her ears. "What big ears, and all that."

The witches nodded.

"You're awfully calm about this," said Torie.

"I'm calm because I agree with them," said Sable, matter-of-factly.

Both Torie and Jasmin stared at the wolf, not quite certain what they had just heard.

"You're okay with this? They are basically using you as bait," said Torie.

Sable nodded slowly. "It was my idea. When Max came to find me in town, to let me know what had happened in the room I was staying in, I saw it as an opportunity to draw Arin out into the open."

"Wolves," said Jasmin, shaking her head. "I will never understand them."

"No, you won't," said Sable, standing up from the small cot she was sitting on and stepping closer to the bars. "And neither will you." She gave Torie a hard stare.

"But you're all playing with fire," said Torie. "To say nothing of the fact this makes you a sitting duck."

"I'm perfectly safe behind these bars. I doubt even Arin could rip through these." She ran her hand up one of the iron bars, giving a tug at them to demonstrate their strength. "Whoever built this jail, built it with shifters in mind. Guess that's one of the benefits of being in a town where the supernatural is commonplace."

"I don't even know what to say anymore," said Torie. "It doesn't have to be this way. All of this could possibly be resolved with a conversation."

"You keep saying that," said Sable, "but it just reinforces what I told you; you don't know wolves. Your man told you that as well. But you aren't listening. You're hearing what you want to hear and filtering out the rest."

She moved back to the cot and sat down. "Let Arin come for me. It's time Max ended this once and for all."

"Are you forgetting that an innocent woman was killed just hours ago?" said Torie. "What about that? Is Max's vendetta against his brother worth more bloodshed?"

Sable's hardened look broke and her face softened for a moment.

"I am truly sorry for what happened to that woman. She was in the wrong place at the wrong time and did not deserve what happened to her. All the more reason to end this sooner rather than later." Her face hardened again, and she looked away from the women.

"Come on, Torie," said Jasmin, pulling her friend by the

elbow. "This isn't getting us anywhere. We need to go get ready for the meeting tonight."

Torie looked at Jasmin, who gave her a slow nod while not breaking eye contact. There was something she wanted to say, but not in front of Sable.

Once they were outside, they looked around for Fionna and found her standing next to the car.

"What is happening with them?" said Torie, when she was sure they were out of hearing range of Sable. "I mean, Elric is not even listening, Max is going all *Braveheart* on us, and Sable...well, I never knew her, but she didn't strike me as the type to just throw in with a half-baked plan like this."

"Not sure what happened, but I'm betting it's the pack mentality setting in," said Fionna, casually.

"What do you mean?" asked Jasmin.

"Werewolves are pack creatures. They behave completely differently when they are in their pack than they do individually. Max and Elric together aren't enough to trigger it; but add in a third...and now you have the beginnings of a pack. They become very different animals. Another reason they were never allowed to live in Singing Falls."

The thought disturbed Torie, and she knew this was something she would need to address with Elric as soon as she could get him alone.

"How did things go with the crowd?" asked Torie.

"Everything is all set for tonight. I explained what we wanted to discuss, and everyone agreed to meet. They are going to spread the word to the rest of the shifters that want to get involved and everyone will be at your place at seven tonight."

They piled into Jasmin's car, and once the doors were closed, she turned to face Torie.

"Something Sable said caught my attention," Jasmin said. "She mentioned that Alma was in the wrong place at the wrong time."

Torie nodded. "You're right. But what did she mean by that?"

"She was implying that Alma must have stumbled onto something, maybe where Arin is, or...who knows. But something she was doing, got her killed. Maybe her death wasn't just a message being sent to Max. Maybe there was another meaning behind it."

"If that's the case, then Sable knows more than she is telling. Maybe we need to take a closer look at the room she was staying in. See if we can find something before Singing Falls turns into a warzone," said Torie.

Fionna sat silently in the back seat as Jasmin eased the car out of the drive and back towards the bed and breakfast. She spoke up when they pulled into the driveway of the house, the yellow police tape still displayed across the porch of the now-empty establishment.

"Guys, if you don't mind, I think I'll pass on going in there."

"Oh, honey, of course," said Jasmin. "We would not expect you to have to go in there."

"Maybe I'll take Leo and head back to Torie's house. I can start getting things ready for the meeting tonight."

"Great idea. Here, take the car. We can get a ride back when we are ready," said Jasmin, handing the keys over to Fionna.

"No that's okay. We can walk. It won't take that long through the woods, and I could use the fresh air. We will be fine."

"Okay, just be careful. And call if you need anything," said Torie as they all got out of the car. She petted Leo on his head and mentally told him to behave and obey Fionna as they headed towards the back of the bed and breakfast and the tree line that marked the property.

"I hope she's alright," said Torie as they turned back to face the house.

"She's strong. She'll pull through. Right now, we need to focus on finding out what happened in that room. You ready?"

Torie took a deep breath and called up her magic, letting it simmer just beneath the surface. Better to have it and not need it than to need it and not be ready she thought as they ducked under the police tape and pushed open the door to the bed and breakfast.

Chapter Twelve

The inside of the large Victorian that had been converted to a bed and breakfast was eerily quiet. Torie thought she would never really get used to quiet of any space that was typically teeming with people, pets, and just all around ambient noise. Anytime she entered such a place to dead silence, it caused her to go on high alert. Probably a holdover from the time that silence meant potential danger for early humans.

At least magic was a better substitute for human senses. She was confident there was no one in the building as she and Jasmin made their way towards the staircase that would lead them to the second floor.

The bed and breakfast was designed around a tree theme. Trees that were local to the North Carolina mountains to be exact. Each of the guest rooms were named and decorated around the more popular foliage found in the mountains.

There was the Sugar Maple room, the Eastern Hemlock room, the Tulip Poplar, and so on. Sable had been staying in the Red Oak room at the end of the hall. Like most of the suites, it had its own private bath and a large window that overlooked the picturesque woods running behind the property.

Torie and Jasmin pushed open the door and looked around. The furniture was sparse, just a dresser, two night-stands, a rocking chair and a small drop-leaf hutch that could double as a writing desk.

"You take the closet, I'll look through the dresser," said Jasmin.

Torie pushed open the sliding closet door only to find there wasn't much to check. There was a single pair of boots on the floor, and a jacket hanging on the wooden clothes-hangers. She felt along the shelf above the hangers, moving aside a folded blanket and a couple of extra pillowcases.

Nothing.

She lifted the ladies' boots and shook them out before going through the pockets of the black denim jacket.

All empty.

"There's nothing here," she called out. "Sable travels very light. Did you find anything?"

"Nope. There are a couple of tee shirts in the drawer here, but that's about it."

Torie joined Jasmin and helped search the nightstands, but again came up with nothing. Then, they checked under the bed, using the flash on their cell phones to illuminate the space.

They moved over to the area next to the chair where Alma's body had been found, taking care not to step in the pool of dried blood that had seeped out around the body.

Torie was glad Fionna had opted not to come with them. It was bad enough to have lost someone you knew in such a horrific fashion; you certainly shouldn't be expected to revisit the scene of the crime when it was still so raw.

"That leaves the bathroom," said Jasmin.

Together, they went through the small space, opening the medicine cabinet and checking the tiny drawers of the vanity. Again, nothing out of the ordinary.

"It just doesn't make sense," Jasmin said as they walked back into the room. "Why would Alma be here? And is this the wrong place at the wrong time Sable was talking about?"

"Maybe she was in a different room here," said Torie. "Alma could have been visiting someone else and overheard or saw something? I don't know." She scratched her head, trying not to look at the dark stains on the carpet.

But there was something about the whole scene that bugged her. Something was off, but she couldn't quite put her finger on what it was. Until she forced herself to look at the area where they had seen the body before it had been removed.

A light went off in her head and she looked at Jasmin, her eyes lighting up in realization.

"What? What is it?" Jasmin asked.

Torie pointed to the bloodstain on the rug.

"We both saw the body. It was mutilated horribly. But look around; there is no sign of a struggle. The blood was limited to this area around where Alma was lying. There is no cast off anywhere else."

She looked up at the ceiling and took a closer look at the walls.

"Her back was gouged deeply. There should be blood splatter everywhere. Why is it so clean?"

Jasmin snapped a finger. "She wasn't killed here. Her body was dumped here!"

"Exactly," said Torie, looking around. "But how would someone have gotten a body up here without anyone downstairs seeing them?"

Jasmin went to the window and bent down to examine the casing. She pointed to something that Torie had to squint to see.

Unlatching the window, Jasmin raised it to get a better look at the scratches inside the frame. They were deep and long, cutting through layers of white paint to show the natural pine-colored wood beneath.

Jasmin placed her hand against the screen and pushed outward, sending it dropping to the ground below. Then she leaned her head out the window enough to get a glimpse of the siding below the window. There were more long gauges and a couple of streaks of red as well.

"This is how they got her up here. They climbed up the side of the house, carrying her body," said Jasmin.

"Well, I guess that lets us know we are definitely dealing with a werewolf."

"As if the slashed throat and giant claw marks on the body weren't enough," said Jasmin, sarcastically.

"How did everyone miss this?" said Torie. "I mean, where did this medical examiner go to school?"

Jasmin shook her head. "Good old Singing Falls detective work at its best. Honestly, I'm not surprised. But what I am surprised at is Max missing this. He's been nothing but distracted since Sable showed up."

"He's not the only one," said Torie, cutting her eyes away from her friend.

"Hey, don't go fretting about Elric and this she-wolf. You know he only has eyes for you. She is not a threat."

"No, you're right. I mean…they only share a bond that is meant to bring them together and cement their relationship for life. A supernatural bond that says of all the wolves, in all the world, they are meant to be together. Why should that worry me?"

Jasmin reached out to her friend and took her arm. "Hey, this isn't like you. What's going on?"

Torie let out a deep sigh. "Honestly, it's the age thing. I don't know why I'm so bothered by it...but I am. I mean, if he's going to basically stay young and fit while I age into oblivion, how's that fair to him?"

"Or to you, right? I mean, that's what you're saying."

Torie swallowed. "Fine. Is it wrong to want to grow old gracefully with someone? I don't want to be some old bag of bones while he still looks like...well, him."

Jasmin folded her arms. "And what does he think about this? Has he told you he only wants you for the way you look to him now?"

"What? No, of course not. He hasn't said anything about it."

"Well, then it seems to me that's your answer. Looks like he hasn't got a problem with any of this."

Torie didn't answer as she contemplated her friend's words.

"You're thinking like Alma probably did when she was with Fionna. Don't let yourself go down that path."

Torie shook her head, clearing her mind. The mention of Alma's name snapped her back to their current reality.

"You're right. Besides, this isn't what we're supposed to be focusing on right now. If Alma wasn't killed here, then where?"

Jasmin thought for a second.

"The next most obvious place to check would be the library. That seems to be where she spent most of her time, and it's where I saw her last."

"Yes, makes sense," said Torie.

Together, they drove the short distance to the town library and walked up the steps to find the 'closed' sign on the door.

"What kind of car does she drive?" asked Torie, glancing around at the empty parking lot.

"No idea," said Jasmin. "For all we know, she could live close by and just walk everywhere."

That made sense to Torie. Either that, or whoever killed her had the sense to get rid of her vehicle as well.

Torie pried the door open with a bit of magic and they let themselves into the building.

Instantly, the hair on the back of Torie's neck stood up, and she felt goosebumps run down the flesh of her arms. Glancing over at Jasmin, she could tell she was feeling the same thing.

Jasmin's eyes glowed blue as she summoned her magic. Torie followed suit while probing the air for any signs of danger.

They made their way past the reception desk and into the open area of the library, behind which the rows of bookcases began. Before they were able to make their way to the cases, a muffled sound came to them from behind two closed doors on the wall to their left.

There was a small round table with a few stacks of books on it, and a few reading chairs set up flanking it. Behind the chairs were the doors, and judging from the look of them, they appeared to lead to a closet rather than another room.

They approached slowly, Jasmin raising a hand with glowing blue magic as she nodded to Torie. Torie placed her hand on the doorknob and counted to three before quickly opening it.

Jasmin quickly recalled her magic when they realized the source of the noise was a small girl, huddled in the back of the closet, her tiny hands covering her face. She recognized her as the girl who was reading at the table when she met with Alma.

"Hey there, sweetie. You're Maura, right? Remember me? I was here earlier and spoke with Ms. Alma." She held her hand out tentatively towards the girl.

Slowly, Maura removed her hands from her face and looked at Jasmin.

"Yes, my name is Maura. You're the nice one that Ms. Alma was talking to upstairs? I remember you."

"That's right. So you know I'm not going to hurt you. This is my friend, Ms. Torie. Can you say hi to her?"

Maura started to smile and nodded at Torie. "Hello."

Torie smiled in return. "Hello, Maura. It's nice to meet you. Do you want to come out of there?"

The girl peeked out slowly, looking around, her eyes large and frightened. She looked like a scared fawn that had been abandoned in the wild.

Jasmin again reached for the girl, and this time, Maura took her hand and allowed herself to be led out of the closet. Once she was in the room and satisfied she was safe, she threw herself into Jasmin's arms.

"It...it's okay," said Jasmin, more than a little shocked. "You're okay now. How long have you been in there?"

Maura started to cry and spoke softly between sobs. "Since Ms. Alma had her important meeting. Then there were all these terrible noises, but I did what Ms. Alma said and kept still and quiet as a mouse. No matter what I heard, she told me to be as still as a mouse and not come out until she came to get me."

Jasmin exchanged a quick look with Torie as she stroked Maura's hair and patted her on the back.

"Maura, do you know who Ms. Alma was meeting with?" said Jasmin.

The girl shook her head, pulling back enough to wipe her nose on the back of her sleeve.

"No, I was sitting there reading *Watership Down* and suddenly Ms. Alma came to find me. She took me by the hand and told me she had an important meeting and to stay in the closet and be real still."

"So, you never saw who she was meeting? You don't know what they looked like?" said Torie.

"No, I only heard her voice, but I didn't see her," said the little girl.

"Her," said Jasmin, staring at Torie. "You're sure it was a woman?"

Maura nodded. "Um-hm. They were talking and then Ms. Alma took her upstairs to show her something. Then, I heard yelling and ...and..." She couldn't finish but instead began to cry again and buried her face in Jasmin's jacket, her tiny body racked with sobs.

"It's okay, honey. Don't you worry about it." Jasmin took the girl by the shoulders and made her look at her. "Maura, I need to call your mommy or daddy to come pick you up. Can you tell me their phone number?"

The girl wrinkled her brow. "I can't call my mommy because she's at work. She works till really late, so Ms. Alma takes me to her house until my mommy can pick me up later. She works at the hospital helping people."

Jasmin frowned. "Okay. I tell you what. I have a friend who worked at that hospital as well. Maybe she can come stay with you until we can find your mommy." She glanced over at Torie, who already had her phone out and was dialing a number.

She hung up and nodded. "Glen is on her way."

"Maura, a friend of mine is coming to take you to find your mommy. But until she gets here, can you sit here at the table while me and Ms. Torie go upstairs and look around?"

Maura's eyes grew wide with fright, and she clawed at Jasmin's arm.

"No! No, you can't go up there. That's where the monster is!"

"What monster, baby? What are you talking about?" said Jasmin.

"I heard a monster up there with Ms. Alma. It was growling and snarling, and it made Ms. Alma scream. I don't want it to make you scream as well."

Torie looked up the stairs. "Maura, you stay here with Ms. Jasmin. I'm going to take a look around upstairs, and I promise you, nothing is going to hurt me. I'll be back in a minute."

Jasmin gave her a worried look, but then just nodded as she led Maura to one of the chairs.

Torie took a deep breath and summoned her magic, focusing it into a red-orange ball of fire that floated above her hand as she mounted the stairs.

Chapter Thirteen

Halfway up the stairs, Torie began to second-guess her bravery. Little Maura had said the monster was upstairs. Torie knew there were no such thing as monsters; what killed Alma was a werewolf. While that might seem like a monster to the uninitiated, she knew better.

Werewolves were turning out to be worse than imaginary monsters. She shook her head. How could she think that? She was practically living with one. And another one had taken over protectorship of the town. They were good men.

But she had seen up close just what some of them were capable of. She shuddered to think what might have happened to her up on the ridge had Max not been there. It might be her body that was being found, chewed and clawed, instead of the town librarian.

She banished such gruesome thoughts from her mind and continued to the landing at the top of the stairs.

There, she reached out with her magic. She envisioned her power as an extension of her senses, pushing out, filling the space around her. It was like having her own personal radar that would ping when it encountered another presence, alerting her to potential danger.

She listened, waiting for the echoes of her power to return. They confirmed what she hoped; there was no one else on the second floor.

She was alone.

Yet somehow, that thought didn't bring her any comfort. She took a few steps forward, and that was when she felt it.

Her magical radar had locked in on something. Not a being of human or supernatural origin, but something that felt more like a hole. It hit her in waves of nausea; tugging at her until she felt like she was going to be physically sick.

She steadied herself and tried to home in on the source of the discomfort. It was coming from a room directly ahead of her. She approached the room slowly until she was standing just outside the entry. Taking a deep breath, she steeled herself and stepped into the darkened space.

Her fire ball floated ahead of her, lighting the room. She smelled it before she saw it.

Blood. Lots of blood.

The large conference table was awash in it. There were streaks of red dotting the floor and the walls, and she knew that this was where it had happened.

She felt along the wall until her fingers touched the light switch. It felt wet, and when she looked at her hand after clicking it on, her fingers were sticky and dark. She swallowed the bile that rose in her throat and forced herself to look at the carnage around her.

It looked like Alma had put up a struggle. There were pockets of blood all around the space and reading lamps that were strategically placed around the conference table were thrown about the room.

Good for her. Though it was unlikely, Torie hoped that the older woman had landed a few good blows before meeting her end. Walking around the space, she noticed there was a wall of small vaults, only one of which was sitting open.

Inside was an old book, written in a language she could not read. There was blood on the leather binding and some of the pages as well. Flipping through it, she came to a missing section. Not missing as in blank pages but missing as in it had been ripped from the book.

Someone had wanted whatever was in this book. Wanted it bad enough to murder a defenseless librarian to get it.

She looked around, not exactly sure what more she could find. She knew she should call Max. Detective work wasn't her specialty, despite all the hours she had logged watching *Law and Order*, this was something the professionals should handle.

Before calling him, she thought of one last thing. Maybe there was a way for her to see more.

She held out her hands, focusing her magic as she began to chant.

"I call on the powers of the mighty seers,
to pierce the veil and show me what happened here."

Ghostly vapors appeared, crawling across the floor like a living mist. It flowed from all corners of the room before creeping up the sides of the table to swirl on top of it. The mist came together forming a large, opaque ball that broke open and separated, forming a three-dimensional scene that played out like a ghastly mirage before Torie's eyes.

It showed two women arguing, one being the aggressor

and the other trying desperately to calm the situation. There was no sound, but Torie could tell from the body language that one of the women, Alma she guessed, was pleading desperately with the other. No matter how closely she looked, however, Torie could not make out any features of the two women. The mist that created the image was foggy, making them both appear as vague outlines.

One of the women struck the other, a blow that sent her flying across the table. Torie winced at the viciousness of the attack as the aggressor then vaulted across the conference table and continued her attack. She held the librarian by the shirt, silently yelling at the woman.

More blows followed and finally the librarian nodded. She stood on shaky legs and moved to the wall, opening the ghost vault and removing something. She held it out to the other woman. From the shape of the mist, Torie assumed it was the book she had just found. She watched as the librarian flipped through it and showed something to the other person.

The attacker took the book and laid it on the table, staring intently at what was written within. That was when the librarian took the opportunity to pick up one of the lamps and smash it across the intruder's head. It appeared to have little affect and only garnered the librarian another smashing blow that sent her flying against the back wall, only to crumple down to the floor.

That was when the attacker moved to stand over her and appeared to yell something else at the woman. Then, to Torie's horror, she bent down and began swiping at Alma with what appeared to be long talons.

Then, something happened that made Torie gasp out loud. The attacker paused, stopping mid-attack, and half turned away from the librarian. She looked around, and then appeared to look up, directly at Torie. She held up her hand, palm outward facing Torie, and emitted a blinding flash of light.

Torie jumped back, shielding her eyes, and when she refocused, the imagery created in her magical mist was gone. The ghostly vapors faded away, receding into nothingness before her very eyes.

Hurrying out of the room, Torie ran down the stairs to find Jasmin who was trying to entertain Maura.

"See, Maura, I told you nothing would happen to Ms. Torie. She is just fine."

Looking at Torie, she could tell she wasn't just fine, but wasn't about to scare the little girl any more than she already had been.

"Well, this is the place. I found something very interesting," said Torie.

They turned to the sound of approaching footsteps just as Glen walked into the room.

"Sorry, I came as quickly as I could," she said, setting her bag onto the table as she surveyed the two women and the child. "I wasn't sure what exactly you needed, so I grabbed my kit in case anyone was hurt."

Jasmin shook her head. "No, I don't think anyone is hurt. At least not physically." She nodded her head in a direction away from Maura, letting Glen know to follow her so they could chat privately. They stepped away a few paces and Jasmin spoke in hushed tones while Glen stole compassionate glances at the child.

When they returned, Glen dropped to her knees in front of Maura and took the girl's hands.

"Hi, Maura, my name is Glen. How are you?"

Maura smiled sheepishly. "Glen? That's a funny name for a girl."

Glen smiled, nodding in agreement. "You're right. That's exactly what my daddy said to my mama when she picked it out." She glanced from Jasmin to Torie before continuing. "Maura, you know, I used to work at the hospital where your mommy works now. How about I take you there and we can find her? Would you like that?"

The little girl nodded her head vigorously, her mop of curly hair covering her face in her excitement.

Glen stood, taking her by the hand, and headed for the door.

"Don't worry, I'll take good care of her," she said over her shoulder to the two witches.

When they were alone, Jasmin turned to Torie.

"What did you find?"

"Come with me," Torie said, rushing up the stairs.

"Slow down," Jasmin called. "My knees do not like stairs anymore."

Once they gained the landing, Torie led Jasmin to the conference room.

"This is the same room where the town's founding documents are kept," said Jasmin. She took in the scene and was nearly overcome by a sense of loss at the carnage in front of her. "Oh my God, she must have been so terrified."

"I don't think she was," said Torie. "I used a clarity spell to see a recreation of what happened here. She fought back."

"Good for her," said Jasmin, her voice little more than a whisper as she took everything in. "What else did the spell show you?"

Torie told her everything, right up to the point where the attacker appeared to look at her and broke her spell.

Jasmin furrowed her brow, placing her thumb and forefinger against her chin.

"That doesn't seem possible," she said.

"I'm telling you what I saw."

"And I'm not doubting you. I just don't see how it's possible. You were viewing an event that happened in the past. How could someone see that and break it? It would be one thing if you were watching as it happened, but I've never heard of a power like this before."

"Well, the other thing I'm pretty sure of is that whatever that thing was that killed Alma, it wasn't a werewolf."

Jasmin took in deep breath and released it.

"And that complicates things on another level. Let's take a look at the book this thing was after."

They went to the wall where Torie had found the book and retrieved it for study.

"I can't read it," said Torie. "I have no idea what it says."

Jasmin studied the book closely before speaking. She turned it over and examined it from all sides. Peering closely, she ran her hands over faded letters printed on one corner of the front cover.

"What is that?" asked Torie, looking over her shoulder.

"It says Deadman. Strange title for something so old." She opened the book and started poring over the pages. "It's written partially in Hex. But then, there are some parts that are written in something that appears to be part Hex and part…something else."

"Can you make out what the book is about?" Torie asked.

"Yes. It's a grimoire, an ancient book of spells and magic."

Torie swallowed hard, staring at the pages. "Why on earth would something like that be in the town library?"

"I have no idea. But the bigger question is, what was on the pages that someone ripped out?"

She closed the book and picked it up, placing it under her arm.

"Come on, let's get out of here," she said.

Torie glanced at the book. "Are we allowed to just take this? Isn't that like stealing from a crime scene?"

"No one knows it's a crime scene just yet. Besides, this is a library, so technically we are just borrowing a book."

Torie knew better than to try and reason with Jasmin's nebulous reasoning at times like this, so she just agreed and the two of them headed out.

"For once, I don't want to be here when Max and his team arrive," said Jasmin. "He and your boyfriend are in a mood. Better we are not here when he starts asking questions."

On that, they were both in agreement.

"What's our next step?" asked Torie as they headed for the library entrance.

"I think it's time I introduced you to Magda. She might be able to tell us a little more about this. She may even be able to read it."

"Who's Magda?" said Torie.

"She's the oldest witch in Trinity Falls. If we're lucky, she'll be in a talkative mood."

Torie stopped mid-step. "And if we're unlucky?"

Jasmin shrugged. "Well, her nickname is Mad Magda. Like I said, she's old. And powerful. She could either talk to us about this, or she could burn us to ash where we stand. Only one way to find out."

Chapter Fourteen

Magda Ophelia Reese lived at the end of a very long private driveway off Hallows Road. Jasmin was strangely quiet on the drive, answering Torie's questions in the simplest manner possible.

"So why have I never heard of this person before? Is she a close friend of yours?"

"She doesn't come up in conversation and no," was the answer.

"Is she a hex witch, like us?"

"A witch, yes; like us, no."

Torie had so many questions, but she could tell her friend was not feeling very talkative. If anything, waves of apprehension were rolling off Jasmin, and while Torie wanted nothing more than to make her friend feel better, she knew the time would come when she would open up; and when that happened, Torie would be there for her.

In the meantime, she sat silently, fiddling with the gift bag in her hands. Inside was a bottle of whisky. A very nice bottle. Jasmin had said that it would go a long way to getting Mad Magda to open up to them.

Whoever this old witch was, she couldn't be that bad. She had excellent taste in whisky after all.

They made their way down the tree-lined drive that eventually opened up to a small cottage that looked like it was right out of the pages of a fairytale. It was a steep A-frame house with exquisite wood detailing and beautiful hand-carved flowers below each of the rectangular windows. Two brick chimneys rose from each side of the steep roof, and Torie could make out smoke coming from each of them.

They were greeted by the scent of honeysuckle and lilac as they stepped out of the car. There was a white picket fence with green ivy growing up the posts enclosing the small but well-manicured lawn. A stone pathway led from the fence to the large front porch.

Before they reached the gate, Jasmin stopped Torie with a hand on her arm.

"Let me take the lead in getting her to talk and, whatever you do, don't say anything about her gardener."

"What?" Torie replied, genuinely confused.

"You'll see," was all that came back to her.

Together, they passed through the gate and walked up the few steps that led to the porch. The door to the cottage was more intricate woodwork and Torie leaned in close to study it. There were fairy folk and elves, as well as quarter moons and stars carved into the wood. In the center of it was a large iron ring that served as a knocker.

Jasmin lifted the knocker and let it slam once against the door. Then they waited.

After a minute, they heard footsteps on the other side and a male voice called out.

"Who is it?"

"It's Jasmin. I need to speak with Magda."

Another pause.

"She says go away; she isn't speaking today."

Jasmin rolled her eyes and took a deep breath.

"Can you tell her it's important? I found something I think she will want to see."

More pauses.

"She said she isn't speaking today or seeing things." Jasmin opened her mouth to reply, but then held her breath instead, swallowing whatever retort she was about to come out with.

She turned to face Torie with a shrug and started to walk away from the door.

"She says leave the gift," said the male voice.

Again, Jasmin rolled her eyes, took the bag from Torie and placed it on the porch before bashing on the door. She ignored the stare Torie gave her as she turned to walk away.

"What, that's it?" said Torie. We come all the way out here just to be told she isn't speaking today?"

"We'll try again tomorrow," Jasmin said.

"No, we won't," said Torie. She picked up the whisky and lifted the knocker, slamming it against the door multiple times, ignoring the panicked look on Jasmin's face.

"Girl, are you crazy?" said Jasmin, grabbing at Torie's arm.

Before she could pull her away, the wooden door drew back with a creak.

Torie's mouth dropped open at the man who answered the door. He was tall, with piercing purple eyes, a mop of curly jet-black hair, and pointed, elfish ears. He was also very lean with defined muscles that looked like they had been welded onto his upper body. Torie could see this because he was also naked from the waist up. Her gaze trailed down his chiseled frame to a pair of black cut-off shorts that left his equally impressive legs on display.

"How dare you," he said, his purple eyes flashing at the witch.

Torie swallowed and regained her composure.

"We are here to see Magda. It's very important, as Jasmin said, and we aren't leaving until we've spoken with her."

"I told you, she said she isn't speaking today."

"Well obviously she is if she said that to you," Torie replied. She leaned to the side, shouting around the distracting male body. "And if she wants this gift, she had better come speak to us. Otherwise, I'm taking it home and adding it to my collection."

Silence followed as the tall elf stared her down. Then, he cocked his head to one side, half looking over his shoulder.

"She wants to know what your name is."

"Torie. I'm Torie Bliss, and we really need her help with something."

Again, the elf listened to something they could not hear, and then he stepped aside, holding the door open for them to enter.

Torie stepped through followed by Jasmin.

"She says come into the kitchen and have a seat. She will be with you momentarily."

The elf led them into a small eat-in kitchen. There was a square wooden table with a bench on one side and two chairs on the other. A wood-fired stove hulked along one side of the room, on which there were two pots filled with something that smelled divine.

They took a seat on the bench and the elf stood at the

other side of the table, staring intently at them. He crossed his arms, causing his chest to swell in a way that made Torie avert her eyes before she started blushing.

They waited in silence for about five minutes before hearing a light tapping noise coming from the hallway that led out of the kitchen.

The tapping was followed by the figure of a woman as she made her way out of the shadow of the hall and into the kitchen. She was short and thin as she walked into the space, aided by the cane she carried in her right hand.

The elf eased the chair back for her to take a seat, and then slowly slid her up to the table. Torie could see she was old, but how old was something she could not guess.

Magda had long, blue hair that was pulled back in a braid, a braid with various flowers and greenery weaved throughout. Her face was thin and angular, almost hawk-like. She studied the two witches across from her. Eyes that were steel gray stared at them, unblinking.

Jasmin cleared her throat and spoke up.

"Magda, thank you for seeing us. I apologize for—" She stopped as the old woman raised a single hand and stared at Torie.

She didn't speak, but her eyes might as well have been lasers as she locked on her.

A line of cold sweat broke out down Torie's back as she suddenly remembered Jasmin's warning about possibly being reduced to a pile of ashes.

"I'm Torie," she said, trying to banish any shaking from her voice. "I guess I'm the bigmouth that was doing all the shouting. I'm sorry for that, it was quite rude of me. I just… we just need your help with something."

Magda said nothing but let her eyes drop to the bag in Torie's hands.

Torie acknowledged the look by holding it out towards the older woman.

"Oh this…I wasn't really going to keep it. It's for you. I just wanted to get your attention."

Magda looked at the elf, and he reached for the bag, withdrawing its contents. Inside was a bottle of Johnnie Walker Platinum whiskey. Magda arched an eyebrow in approval as the elf retrieved three whiskey glasses from a cabinet and placed them on the table in front of the women. He opened the bottle and poured a perfect two-finger pour in each of the glasses.

Magda claimed hers, swirled it around a bit, breathed in the heavy aroma and took a swig.

"Oh, that's good," she said, delightedly. She gave the elf a nod, and he moved to quickly cap off her glass with a bit more of the amber brew.

The elf then turned his back to place the remaining liquor in the cabinet. Torie didn't mean to stare, but she couldn't help but notice the tattoo on his lower spine that dove into the waistband of his shorts. It looked like the beginnings of a Celtic rune, but she couldn't be sure.

Magda narrowed her eyes. "You see something you like?"

Torie blushed immediately and dropped her gaze to her hands in her lap, remembering Jasmin's warning about the gardener. Wait, was that her gardener?

"Oh no…I'm sorry I didn't mean to stare. Not that I was staring, I mean…I wasn't looking at anything."

Magda leaned in closer to the table, narrowing her eyes further at Torie.

"Why not? Are you saying he's not worthy of your gaze?"

Flustered, Torie wasn't quite sure how to respond to

that. She looked to Jasmin for help that wasn't coming. She swallowed hard, worried that if her cheeks got any hotter Magda wouldn't have to worry about burning her to the ground; she'd do it herself.

Just then the old woman burst out in laughter, slapping her hand on the table hard enough to draw a jolt and slight gasp from both Torie and Jasmin.

"Oh, I'm just joshing you, girl," said Magda. "Of course, you can look at ole Jinn, there. He's hotter than newly paved asphalt in August. Why do you think I have him around?"

Torie opened her mouth to speak but thought better of it. Magda kept staring, which told her the old witch was waiting for an answer.

"Um, I suppose to help you around the house and keep up the lawn?" Torie said.

"Ha!" Magda shouted, slapping the table again. "Are you saying I'm not capable of cleaning up after myself or weeding my own garden? Is that what you're saying now?"

"Of course not...I mean, you look more than capable."

"Damn right I am. I keep Jinn around because he is young and beautiful and when you get to be my age, you have to surround yourself with youth. Otherwise, old age sets in. That's why you don't see men hanging around with the likes of..." She looked over and jerked her head towards Jasmin. Torie's surprised reaction drew another hoot from the old witch.

"And that I'm not joshing you about. You'll see; as you get even older, get yourself something pretty to look at around the house. Plus, you'd be surprised at what the young ones can learn from us, isn't that right, Jinn?"

The elf turned to face the table and smiled, nodding.

Dimples, thought Torie, he has dimples on top of everything else.

"But I hear you have a werewolf at home," said Magda. "I suspect that will keep you young for quite some time to come." She lifted the glass to her lips once again. "Well, young in spirit at least." Her eyes sparkled after that last remark, and Torie frowned at the old woman, wondering just what she knew.

"But enough about all that,' said Magda. "I'm sure there must be something very pressing that would bring you banging on my door like a lunatic at this ungodly hour. So, what is it?"

"I'm sorry, I didn't think it was that late…" Torie started before being cut off by Jasmin.

"Apologies for visiting at such a late hour, Magda, but we really do need your help."

She reached into the satchel she wore slung across her body and withdrew the leather-bound grimoire they had taken from the library. She laid it carefully on the table and pushed it over to Magda.

"We were hoping you could tell us a little bit about this."

The old witch looked at the book without touching it.

"Where did you find this?" Magda asked.

"It was in the town library. In the records vault," replied Jasmin. "It's written in Hex, but then there are parts that are in a language I can't read."

"This book was under the watch of a protector," said Magda. "How did you get it?"

A protector? This was the first time Torie had heard the term.

"I don't know anything about a protector," said Jasmin.

Magda rolled her eyes and sighed as if she were dealing with preschoolers.

"The librarian, where is she?" asked the old witch.

Torie and Jasmin exchanged glances before Torie spoke up.

"She's dead. She was killed by…something. We aren't sure what."

Hearing those words, Magda drew herself up in her seat, her body becoming rigid. Her gray eyes flashed and, in the distance, Torie was certain she heard the roll of thunder.

"I'm sorry," said Torie. "Did you know Alma?"

"She was my sister," said Magda. Again, her eyes flashed, and this time there was no mistaking the sound of approaching thunder.

Jinn hurried to stand beside the old woman, lightly placing a hand on her shoulder.

For a second, Magda looked at the elf, her dark eyes growing less angry, and she seemed to calm down just a bit.

"Magda, I am sorry for your loss," said Jasmin. "You know that we are going to find who did this, and when we do, they will pay. You have my word on that."

Magda's features grew hard as she regarded Jasmin. "Where is her body?"

"She's being held at the medical examiner's office. They need to finish—" But before Jasmin could complete her sentence, Magda turned to Jinn and gave him a hard nod. The big elf turned and rushed out of the house.

"What…what just happened?" asked Torie.

"I sent Jinn to retrieve her body," said Magda.

Her sudden calm demeanor should have put Torie and Jasmin at ease; instead, it had the opposite effect on the two witches.

"Now, back to your problem," said Magda, looking over the book.

"Welin a nutshell, we are trying to prevent a turf war from happening here in Singing Falls between werewolves. We found a document that alleges Singing Falls was possibly a sanctuary town, a place where physical violence by super-naturals was against the law. And breaking that law carried magical ramifications. We want to recast the spell that would limit what shifters can do when it comes to causing harm in the town," said Jasmin.

"Well, we are considering that as an option," said Torie, quickly.

The look that passed between them wasn't missed by Magda.

"We found a document that detailed the decree," said Jasmin. "What we don't know is, was the spell actually cast? Fully? Partially? Not at all? Then, we learned that the lib—your sister—was…"

"Murdered," said Magda. "You can say it. It's what happened." Her voice was hard, and she had to swallow her emotions as she said the words.

"You know, this may not be the right time to do this," said Torie. "You need to deal with the shock of what has just happened. You need to grieve."

Magda stared at Torie, her gaze softening somewhat.

"Thank you, dear. But there will be time for that later. You think that whatever you uncovered regarding this spell to limit shifter behavior was somehow linked to my sister's death?"

Torie nodded. "We can't be certain, but there are pages from this book that the killer seemed to be after when Alma was attacked."

Jasmin reached over and pointed to the word Deadman that was inscribed on the cover.

"Do you know what this means?" she asked.

Magda looked at the word and then back up at Jasmin.

"It's a name. An old surname. This is the author of this grimoire."

Of course. It made sense in a way.

"I don't know any witches by that name and lineage," said Jasmin.

Magda waved her hand. "Of course you do." Her eyes twinkled as they settled on Torie. "That name is infamous in certain magical circuits. But over the generations, for some very unsavory reasons, it had to be changed to a new surname.

"Bliss."

Chapter Fifteen

Torie stared at the old witch, the confusion in her eyes slowly giving way to fear.

"But that's my last name," she said. "Are you saying I am somehow related to the witch who wrote this?"

Magda nodded before opening the book and carefully turning through the delicate pages.

"This is indeed written in the old Hex language; but there are parts of it that are from the ancient language of Coptic," said Magda.

"I've never heard of that language before," said Jasmin.

"It is pre-Arabic. It's dead now. Although I believe there are still some older, early Christian manuscripts that can be found written in the language."

"Why would the church have documents written in the ancient language of Hexes?" asked Jasmin.

"There is a reason the church used to burn witches. At one time, they had a lot in common," said Magda. "That is, until men took over the church..." She waved her hand in dismissal. "But that's not something we need to discuss right now. This book…the spells contained, are very interesting."

"How so?" asked Torie.

"Most of the spells I'm seeing here are reversals. Meaning they are a way to break the spells cast by another witch."

"Wait," said Torie, turning to Jasmin. "You always said that only the witch who cast the spell could break it."

"That is a common misunderstanding," said Magda. "Once cast, the spell can only be broken by the witch who cast it; that is true. However, another witch, one who is skilled enough, can cast a spell that would interact with it in a negative way. Not reverse it; but maybe alter it. It's very difficult and dangerous, but it can be done."

"And you're saying this grimoire is dedicated to that?" asked Jasmin.

"For the most part," Magda replied, flipping through the pages slowly. "There are a few other spells, as well as some interesting potion building ingredients; but for the most part, it is a treatise on undoing magic."

"What purpose would someone have for that?" asked Jasmin.

"The spells inscribed within this tome are used in battle-magic. A lost art if you ask me." Magda huffed, turning away from the book.

"So, we have no idea what kind of spell reversal could have been on the pages that were stolen," said Torie.

"One guess," replied Jasmin. "A way to undo or maybe even block, the sanctuary spell we were considering casting on the town."

Magda was nodding. "That would be my guess. That would also be why Alma would have fought so hard to protect it." She glanced away from the two of them at the mention of her sister's name.

"I'm sorry to bring this up now, but why wouldn't Alma have told me this book existed?" asked Jasmin. "She showed me the documentation about the casting of the original spell…it would have been nice to have this one as well." She shook her head in sadness. "And if she had given it to me, she might still be alive."

"Do you have the original spell you speak of?" asked Magda. "May I see it?"

"Of course," said Jasmin, fishing in her satchel again to hand the parchment over to Magda.

The old witch glanced over it, her eyes sweeping down the page until they stopped, fixating on one portion. She looked up at Jasmin, questioningly.

"This name, the one signed in red…are you aware of who this is?" asked Magda.

Jasmin nodded. "Yes, she was one of my ancestors."

"Indeed," Magda replied. She drummed her fingers slowly on the table, deep in thought. "I know why Alma would not want you to have this grimoire."

"You do?" asked Torie. "Can you tell us? It may help us with what is going on in town."

Magda reached for her drink and took a long draw, nearly emptying the glass. Despite herself, Torie was impressed. This woman could probably drink her under the table any day of the week.

"Your ancestor—" she pointed to Jasmin, "—was one of the original settlers of Singing Falls. She created the sanctuary spell. She did not properly document the spell, but it hints at it here in the document."

Magda, pointed to the cabinet where Jinn had left the

whisky. Jasmin opened it, took out the bottle, and poured her another shot, which she downed almost immediately.

"Your ancestor, Torie Deadman—"

"I'm sorry, my name is Bliss," Torie interrupted.

Magda narrowed her gray eyes. "Oh no. Trust me, you are a Deadman." She looked from Torie to Jasmin and back again. "Your ancestor was the one who countered the spell. Who reversed it, for whatever reason." She looked away, unable to meet their gaze.

Jasmin seized on the moment.

"Magda...what are you not telling us? You know something, don't you?"

Magda's eyes hardened and her back stiffened. "I know many things, girl. More than you'll ever learn."

Her gaze softened slightly as she stared at her now-empty glass.

"Forgive my little outburst. I think it's starting to hit me that my sister is...is..." She didn't finish the sentence. She didn't have to.

"We are so sorry for your loss," said Torie, leaning in. "But I am afraid that Alma may only be the first in a number of casualties if we don't stop this impending war between the werewolves. If there is something, anything you can tell us; please help us."

Magda took a deep breath and stared at the two women.

"You are friends, yes? I can see that you care deeply for one another."

Torie nodded, a little confused. "Yes, we are. I consider Jasmin to be my closest friend in the world." She looked up at Jasmin and smiled. "Even if we don't quite see eye to eye on this matter. But what does that have to do with anything?"

Magda shrugged. "Maybe nothing. Maybe everything. I know the history of your ancestors. The one who was involved in the town founding, and the one who wrote this grimoire." She tapped her forefinger on the leather-bound book. "They were not friends."

The finality of her tone shook the two witches, and their slumped into the chairs.

"What do you mean they weren't friends?" said Torie.

"Hmmm. What do you know about the witch covens that originally settled in these parts?" asked Magda.

Jasmin shook her head. "Not much. We both grew up without the guidance of our mothers, so there wasn't a lot to learn about what was handed down to us."

"Interesting," said Magda. "You both have come into your power without the benefit of knowing about your ancestors. That might explain it."

"Explain what?" asked Torie. She was struggling to not use a sterner tone with the old witch, but as patient as she was, she had her limits.

"Just like those wolves you hang out with have their packs, witches have covens. Our version of pack. For the most part, the covens tolerated one another, especially in the early days. That was the time when we all had a common enemy. Man. But we were still all born into different covens and in this area, the covens were named after the seasons. Your ancestor, Jasmin, was from the winter coven. You, Torie, were born into the summer coven. Right away, that tells me you were diametrically opposed to one another. You are opposites. And not the kind that attract one another."

Torie held up her hand. "Something tells me we are going to need a drink to hear the rest of this. May I?"

Magda nodded, and Torie retrieved the bottle Jasmin

had placed back in the cabinet. She poured them each a drink, refilling Magda's as well.

Jasmin started to protest, nodding at the old witch and then the drink.

"Oh pssh," said Magda. "Don't be winking and nodding my way. I've been holding my liquor longer than the two of you have been sipping on juice cups. I'm fine." She picked up the glass and took another sip to echo her point.

"So anyway, as you were saying?" prompted Torie.

"From what I know, your ancestors were bitter rivals. Each trying to grow their coven into the most powerful in the area. Story is, your ancestors hated one another. One cast the spell, the other reversed it. And that reversal led to the death of the winter witch—Jasmin's ancestor."

Jasmin sat her glass down forcefully.

"Are you intimating that my ancestor killed Jasmin's? That isn't possible."

Magda arched a single eyebrow. "Oh no? Why not? Because all witches are supposed to be lovey-dovey and care about one another? Try telling that to the witches who live down in Trinity Falls. See how far that gets you."

Jasmin looked at Torie and rolled her eyes.

"Even if what you're saying is remotely true," said Jasmin, "what does that have to do with us in this moment, here and now."

"Because your ancestors were powerful witches," said Magda. "Magic flows down the timeline through you. We draw our power from our ancestors' spirits. And spiritual energy can be a two-sided blade."

Jasmin didn't say anything, but Torie could practically see her thoughts racing. She also saw something else.

Something Magda had just said stirred fear in Jasmin.

Magda saw it too.

"You understand what I'm saying, even if she doesn't," she said to Jasmin. "Tell me; what is really going on here? Why the sudden impetus to return Singing Falls to its sanctuary status?"

"Because we've had a request," said Torie, softly. "One that has led us on the path to where we are now."

"Does that request have to do with a man?" asked Magda.

Torie felt a jolt of electricity run up her spine as she looked at the old witch. "Why would you ask that?"

"Just wondering. There is always a reason for a divide among our kind. Covens kept to themselves, but something drove your ancestors to seek one another out. Find one another, and that led to one killing the other. That forever divided the lines between your two covens. You should not be together now. Your mothers would never have allowed it."

"I knew Torie's mother," said Jasmin. "She was a great woman and a hell of a witch. I was lucky enough to call her my friend."

"Perhaps," said Magda, "but had your mother been around, I am willing to bet that she would not have been friends with Torie's mother. She would have stopped the two of you ever getting to know one another."

"That's not true!" said Torie. She was getting angry, and she could feel the magic swelling within her. "Are you saying that our parents knew about their heritage…their coven origins? If they did, then why would my mother have befriended Jasmin? Why would she have introduced us?"

Magda had no answer for her, and she simply stared at Torie in response.

"That isn't for me to answer. All I can do is let you know what transpired in the past between your respective covens."

"How do you know all of this?" asked Jasmin. "I mean, are there witch archives or something?"

"Of course there are," said Magda. "Witches are great historians and, at some point, everything in our history has been written down."

Jasmin stared unblinkingly at her. "I was kidding. But if that's the case, where can we find these archives?"

Magda looked away, letting out a long sigh. "That is something only a protector could answer. They are the guardians of such knowledge."

Torie saw Jasmin start to ask a question and waved her off. Whatever else they may need, they had to remember that this woman had just lost her sister.

Nothing good would come from pressing any issues regarding that.

"Thank you, Magda. You have given us so much to think about," said Torie. "I believe we should be leaving now."

She stood and nodded at Jasmin. Silently, they placed their cups in the sink and turned to leave the room.

"Jasmin, Torie," said Magda as she stood. "When you find out who did this to my sister. I want to know."

Jasmin could only nod as they left the house.

Her phone beeped as they were about to climb into the car. She read the text, her eyes growing wide.

"What is it?" asked Torie.

"It's Max. Apparently, Elion just broke Sable out of jail."

Chapter Sixteen

The police station was a beehive of activity.

Torie and Jasmin entered the chaos, pushing their way through the police officers, a couple of crime scene investigators snapping pics, and a member of the janitorial staff who seemed to be dazed and confused as he sat in one corner of the lobby scratching at his head.

Whereas they would have normally been stopped well before they could enter the holding area, this time no one seemed to say a word as they made their way into the back of the building where Max and Elric stood talking.

"What happened?" Torie asked, placing a hand on Elric's arm. "Are you okay?"

"Yeah, we're fine,' said Elric. "But Max's jail cell has seen better days." He nodded to the cell that had held Sable when they were last visiting.

Not only were the bars on the door bent outward, but the entire metal door had been ripped out of its foundation and cast aside.

Jasmin stepped into the room, careful to avoid the

rubble of concrete that had been ripped free from the floor along with the door.

"Wow," she said appreciatively as Torie moved to stand next to her.

"Oh yeah, and I'm fine too...thanks for asking," said Max, bitterly.

Torie's brow furrowed, and she immediately felt guilty for ignoring the sheriff. Before she could apologize, Jasmin huffed.

"It's not like we didn't tell you. You knew Elion was not going to just accept this, didn't you?"

Torie stepped in before Max could reply. She saw a vein stand out along the side of his forehead and knew the were-wolf was in no mood to play this evening.

"Were you here when this happened? How did he get in?" asked Torie.

"We were both here," replied Max. "We were in the office, discussing your little meeting you're having tonight, and suddenly, we heard this wrenching sound. He came in through the back door." He led them around the hall corner to the back entrance used by the deputies and staff.

It was a large, solid metal door with a sophisticated, state-of-the-art locking mechanism that kept it secure. It had to weigh at least a half ton, and it now lay in the hallway, about six feet from its frame. There was a fist-sized indent in the center of the steel.

"He did this?" Jasmin raised her brows. "Just punched the door off its hinges like this?"

Elric was nodding. "By the time we got back here, he was standing at the cell speaking to Sable. They stopped talking as soon as we entered the room."

Max shook his head. "Most of my men had already left for the day. There were only a few left in the building and they responded, weapons drawn. He dropped them like they were a bunch of paper dolls. I've never seen anything move that fast. One minute he was standing by the cell door, the next he was in the center of the room having scattered my deputies."

"Will they be okay?" Jasmin asked.

"A few bruises, but they'll survive."

"I thought you had shifters working for you?" Torie said.

"I do. And he knew that as well. He took them out before they could turn. Quick and easy like."

"We knew there was no point in trying to fight, so we tried to reason with him," said Elric. "But he wasn't hearing it. We told him Sable was safe where she was, and we had a plan to deal with Arin. But it fell on deaf ears."

"He gave us a warning not to get in his way, then, he just pulled the door off, put an arm around Sable, and sped away. No way even we could have kept up with him," added Max.

"Well, not that I would say I told you so, but this was a bad idea from the start," Torie said.

"You might not say it, but I would," said Jasmin, eying the two wolves. "Any idea where they might have gone?"

"None," answered Max. "Sun just went down completely, so he could be anywhere with her by now."

Torie looked at her watch. Elion had struck just as the sun was beginning to fade behind the tall trees that blocked the jail. He had to have been waiting in the forest for the right moment to strike. But where would he have taken Sable?

She had an idea and she hoped she was wrong.

"Well, there is nothing we can do here," said Torie. "We need to get back to my place for the town meeting. Looks like you're going to have to miss it, Max; I'm sure you'll have a lot of cleaning up, and covering up, to do around here."

The sheriff narrowed his eyes. "Yeah, well I'm sure you know where I stand on the matter. And just to be certain, I give Elric permission to cast my proxy vote in the matter if it comes down to it."

Torie couldn't bring herself to look at her boyfriend as she nodded and headed out the destroyed back door.

"Elric, I'll see you in about an hour at the house," she called over her shoulder.

"I'll be there," he said pointedly as they made their way back around the front of the building to their vehicle.

The lights were all on at Torie's house as they arrived. Luckily, no one from town had arrived just yet and that gave Torie time to shower and gather up Leo in her arms as she returned to the kitchen where Fionna was hard at work setting out glasses, plates, and cutlery.

On the large kitchen island were stacked boxes of delivered pizza.

Torie frowned. "Pizza? This is what we have for everyone?"

"Well, it's not like I had time to create one of your gourmet spreads," said Fionna. "Or the know-how." She smiled and took one box off the stack to open it, revealing a large pie covered in cheese and meats. "Besides, this will go a long way in making everyone feel comfortable. I even have some that are vegan for those of us who aren't particularly fond of meat."

Torie eyed the pile of carbs and cholesterol suspiciously but only nodded to her friend in agreement. "If you say so."

She placed Leo on the floor and went to the refrigerator to retrieve some cubes of raw steak she had saved for him.

"Have you ever tried cooking that first before giving it to him?" Fionna watched as the little dragon dove headfirst into the plate of meat Torie sat before him.

"Not really. When I first started feeding him, he was pretty finicky about what he would and would not eat. The only thing I could get him to keep down was raw meat."

Fionna wrinkled her nose at the sight of him tearing into the flesh.

"I just wonder because he breathes fire and all. Maybe dragons in the wild barbecue their food before they eat it. Why else would he be able to breathe fire?"

"Oh, I don't know...maybe to pillage villages. It certainly came in handy when we were dealing with those two old soul traders," said Torie. She didn't like thinking about her pet reducing two humans to ash; even if they did have it coming and would probably have killed Torie and her friends had Leo not done what he did.

"Well, that sounds like what a wild, savage dragon would do," said Fionna. "If he's going to live here in Singing Falls, he can't go around torching the citizens."

Torie had to admit that she had a point. Her bond with Leo was growing stronger by the day. All she could hope was that he was taking on her personality as he aged.

"Hey, where's Jasmin?" Torie queried.

"Oh, she went on a quick beer run. She should be back any minute now."

She tilted her head as her ears picked up something that Torie could not hear.

"Sounds like our first guests have arrived. I'll let them in, you finish up with your little carnivore." She wiped her hands on a dishtowel hanging from the oven door and headed out to greet their guest. Sure enough, no sooner had she left the kitchen than Torie heard the doorbell chime.

"Okay, you. I think it's time we put you back in the study." She reached for Leo and placed him on her shoulder as she started to head down the back hall towards her private office. She stopped, relishing in the emotions the dragon was giving off.

He was content and happy. A little belch, accompanied by a few wisps of smoke exiting his nostrils, told Torie he was also very full. She reached up and held him in her hand, looking down at him.

"If I let you stay out, I want you to be on your best behavior. Understand?" She pushed a mental image of her expectations to the little dragon and felt his response float to her mind. It wasn't like she heard actual words from the dragon...more like an affirmation that he understood and would do his best to comply.

"Fine," she said, placing him back on her shoulder. Everyone else had their pets and loved showing them off; why should this be any different for her?

Not that she thought of Leo as a pet. She felt deep down that he did not belong to her. It was more like he was spending time in her presence while he decided what he wanted to do; or become.

Either way, she wasn't going to keep him locked away from her while she was entertaining in her own home. These weren't humans; they were shifters of all kinds and beings that were used to the supernatural.

Seeing a dragon shouldn't be that big a deal to them, right?

She snapped out of her thoughts just as Fionna's voice preceded her into the kitchen. Behind her, a man and a woman entered the room, smiling as they marveled at the beautiful home they had been welcomed into.

"And this is our host for the night," said Fionna, gesturing to Torie. "Torie Bliss, meet Devon and Meryl Wilkes. They have that beautiful little cottage just off Evergreen. They are both fox shifters and are very interested in what you have to say tonight." She did a double take as she caught sight of Leo and then motioned to him as well. "Um, this…this is Leo. Torie's…cat." She looked at Torie, eyes wide, waiting for her to acknowledge the cat sitting on her shoulder.

"Cat?" said Meryl, smiling intently at the little dragon. "Why, that's a dragon if I've ever seen one! Well, I mean, I've never seen one…but I'm sure that's a dragon." Wonder filled her voice and she looked at Torie questioningly as she held up a hand towards Leo. "May I?"

Torie smiled and nodded.

"Of course. I'm not sure how he'll respond…this is the first time he's been around company."

To their delight, Leo sniffed at the shifter's hand, and then offered a tiny lick at the finger. Then, he lowered his head and rubbed it up and down her palm.

Torie breathed easier as she realized that at least one thing was going to go right tonight.

More voices echoed through the house as Jasmin entered, trailed by a few more people that Torie recognized from town. At Jasmin's shoulder, a large box of beer floated along beside her. With a wave of her hand, Jasmin settled it on the island next to the pizza. Then, with another flourish, she ordered the bottles out of the box and had them settle in the large, silver tub of ice that sat opposite the pizza.

She smiled at Torie as she took the empty cardboard

box and placed it on the deck before returning to the kitchen.

"What?" she said in response to Torie's gaze. "Everyone here knows we are witches. What's the big deal? Besides, in case you hadn't noticed, you have a dragon sitting on your shoulder."

Torie ignored her as she made her way around the room, introducing herself to people she did not know, and reacquainting herself with those she had only met in passing.

As her house began to fill up, she moved into the large great room, and Fionna and Jasmin began to usher the townsfolk in behind her. Everyone seemed to be oohing and aahing over little Leo, so when a hush descended over the crowd, she turned to see what else had captured everyone's attention.

That was when she saw them. Sable and Elion had walked into the room, the sea of people parting to let them pass. They walked into the great room and stood front and center.

"I'm sorry," said Elion, "has the meeting started without us?"

Chapter Seventeen

Torie locked eyes with the vampire.

"I had a feeling you'd be here," she said.

"Well, you did say it was an open meeting for all members of the supernatural community," he replied.

"You're not a member of this community," came a voice from one of the people assembled in the room.

"That's right," added another. "Vampires should not be here."

"I may not be a member of your community, but make no mistake, what is happening here affects me." Elion reached to his side and took Sable's hand in his. "In more ways than you can know."

Jasmin walked calmly up to stand next to Torie.

"Should we call Max?" she asked, not taking her eyes off the vampire.

"I don't think so. I have a feeling word will get to him soon enough. But in the meantime, let's move on with things."

"Your call. Hey, how's Fionna?" Jasmin asked, nodding

her head in the direction of their friend. "She seems on edge again, the way she's staring at Elion. How's she dealing with what happened to Alma?"

"She hasn't talked about it. You know how she is with stuff like that. If she doesn't bring it up soon, maybe we should," said Torie.

She cleared her throat and smiled at the room full of people sitting and standing around in her house.

"Thank you, everyone, for coming out to discuss a very important topic. But before we get started, I would like to formally welcome you all to my home and give a special thank you to Fionna for helping to organize this and for making sure there was plenty of food for everyone tonight." She smiled warmly at Fionna and clapped lightly, as did everyone else. "I couldn't have done this without you, my friend."

Fionna blushed and nodded but didn't say anything; her gaze gradually resettling on Elion and Sable.

"So, I don't know how this is supposed to work; I've never actually been to a town meeting before, let alone ran one. But I say we just jump right into things and get on with the matter at hand."

Before she could go further, a slender woman sitting on one of her loveseats stood up. She was wringing her hands together and her face was filled with worry.

"First, how do we know that anything we discuss here tonight stays here? I have a family, and I don't want to be marked for retaliation by... werewolves." She almost whispered the last word as she looked around the assemblage, her cheeks flushing red at the sight of Sable and Elric.

"Because you have my word," said Torie. "Everyone here tonight is just as concerned about how things will go as you are. No one is coming after anyone for speaking their truth."

"That's easy for you to say! You're a witch; you can protect yourself. I'm a rabbit shifter...what can I do against those monsters?" This time it was a man who spoke up from the back of the room.

A murmur passed through the crowd, most in agreement with the statement.

A woman that Torie had first met in the kitchen stood up. "May I speak?"

"Yes, of course. Meryl, right?"

The woman nodded, concern clouding her pretty features.

"As one of the oldest members of this community, I think we all owe you a debt of gratitude for all that you and your friends have done for us since you moved to this town. But I think we also all recognize that there have been other changes that have occurred that maybe we aren't all so crazy about. There are wolves living among us now. And..." She glanced at Elion and quickly looked away when he tried to meet her gaze. "Other supernaturals that have never been allowed to live in this town before.

"That, coupled with the rash of violence that has washed over our once peaceful town, have made it clear that things are changing. Life as we knew it here in Singing Falls has taken a turn. I think it's time we accept that maybe things aren't going back to the way they were."

Devon, who stood next to her, spoke up. "We pride ourselves on being a community that values inclusiveness and diversity. Doesn't that mean we value everyone? Who are we to start saying who can and who can't be part of this community?"

A murmur of dissension flowed across the gathering.

"I agree. But I say we need to maintain some degree of separation when it comes to killers." This came from somewhere in the back of the room to a chorus of nods.

"But are we saying every werewolf that comes to town is a killer? What about Max? Everyone in this room has accepted him as the new sheriff, and have been grateful to have him," asked Torie, speaking over the voices. "Who are we to decide who can move here? And if so, why stop at werewolves? What about tiger shifters? Or bear shifters for that matter?"

A large, burly man stepped forward, holding a baseball cap in his hands.

"I am a bear shifter, and I would not hurt a fly. I have been a member of this community for many years, and I know everyone in this room. There is not violence in my heart, I can assure you of that."

"And I'm not saying there is," said Torie. "I'm just pointing out the fact that wolves aren't the only carnivores out there."

No one spoke until Elric stepped forward to address the crowd.

"Most of you know who I am. And for those who do not, I am a werewolf." There were a few audible gasps as the room settled into silence. "I have seen the fear in the eyes of shifters when they first hear what I am. I've seen some of you cross the street to avoid me while walking around town.

"I have not been here long, but I can say that I would give my life protecting everything in this town before I would hurt an innocent." He didn't need to look at Torie for her to know he was referencing her. "But Meryl is right. Things are changing here in Singing Falls. There are bad elements that will come here; that is inevitable—"

A woman's frightened voice cut him off. "Bad elements? What kind of bad elements? That was never a concern before you and the sheriff moved to town."

More agreement rolled through the gathering.

"And now you've brought a vampire in as well," said the same woman. "If this is allowed, then Singing Falls will be the next Trinity Cove. Darkness and death will be everywhere."

At the mention of Singing Falls' sister town, more voices rose, displacing any sense of calm that might have been prevalent moments before.

"That won't happen here," said a strong voice from the very back of the room.

Everyone turned just as Max walked into the room. He held his sheriff's hat in his hands as he pushed through the crowd, looking anyone that faced him in the eyes.

"It won't happen because I won't let it," he said. "But Elric is right. And so are all of you. I hear the fear in your voices, and I understand it." He moved to stand next to Torie. "I used to feel that fear as well. Elric and I moved up here from Trinity Cove. We know what it's like to be afraid of something that goes bump in the night. In that town, werewolves were not at the top of the food chain; so the things that went bump in the night brought a special kind of fear, even for us.

"But that won't happen here."

"And what's to stop it?" called a voice.

He looked over at Torie and Jasmin, smiling slightly at them. "Well, other than myself and these two women here…everyone in this room. The fact that all of you are here tonight is a testament to how much you love your town and one another. You would never let Singing Falls turn into another Trinity Cove.

"But having said that, you all have heard what happened to Alma, am I right? That was a shame, and one that I feel personally responsible for. But because of that, I promise you that I will do everything in my power to see to it that you never have to be afraid to walk these streets; in midday, or at midnight."

A man, small of frame with eyes that appeared to be jet-black orbs, stepped forward. "Sheriff, is it true that there is a pack of werewolves headed to town? Out for bloody revenge against you and Elric?"

He was not someone Torie recognized from town, and she hadn't seen him come into the house earlier. "Who's that?" she whispered to Jasmin.

"His name is Walter Fees. He's a badger shifter; lives out by the old paper mill. Typically sticks to himself. I'm surprised he made it out for this."

Torie didn't need to ask how she felt about the man, her tone told her everything she needed to know.

Max eyed the shifter closely before answering.

"That may be true," he said. "But we will deal with anything that comes to town with ill intent. I can assure you of that."

The badger shifter narrowed his black eyes. "Way I hear it, they are already here. I heard you and one of the witches already ran into one of them that tried to kill you both. Is that true?"

Max swallowed hard. "We ran into a bit of trouble up on the ridge, yes. But it wasn't anything we couldn't handle. As I said, I can promise you—"

He was cut off by Walter yet again. "And is it true that the leader of the pack invading our town is none other than your brother? And that he wants you, your buddy over there, and that new she-wolf that probably killed Alma, dead?"

The hush that followed his words was mixed with apprehension and fear. Eyes darted about the room, settling on Elion and Sable.

Max's eyes flared dangerously. "You seem to know an awful lot for someone who never comes into town. Care to share your source, Walter?"

The badger pursed his lips and met Max's steely gaze with his own.

"That's not important," Walter replied. "Instead, maybe everyone would like to hear the witches' plan to handle all of this."

He turned his gaze to Torie and Jasmin, the corners of his mouth slowly changing to a smirk.

"It's simple," said Jasmin, speaking out for the first time. "Singing Falls was meant to be a literal sanctuary town. We have found the decree in the founding fathers' documents. What that means, is that everyone is meant to live here without fear of violence enacted upon them by…certain elements."

"And what exactly do you mean by 'certain elements?'" asked Elion. His voice was calm and monotone as he directed the question at Jasmin.

She narrowed her eyes at the interruption but was nonplussed by the vampire.

"That's easy, Elion. I mean vampires and werewolves. Is there a distinction between the two in the eyes of this decree?"

Her bluntness startled the group and murmurs began circulation through the townsfolk.

She held up her hand in order to continue. "But that doesn't mean werewolves or vampires can't be residents or move into town. It simply means they cannot commit acts of aggression against any law-abiding member of the community. There is a spell we have uncovered that was meant to be part of the foundation of Singing Falls. It will enforce the no-violence edict."

"How does it work?" asked another member of the assemblage.

"Well, once cast, if it is violated by a werewolf, then that wolf would be stripped of their ability to shift. They would be locked in their natural form forever."

No one spoke, but Torie could sense the unease coming from everyone. Elric had crossed his arms and was shifting his body weight from one foot to the other.

"And vampires? How would it work against us?" asked Elion.

"That is yet to be determined," said Jasmin. "But since there are no vampires living here—"

"There was one," Fionna said, "Arnold. He hid it from a lot of people, but he was a vampire. And he also killed a lot of the members of this community."

"I think there are a lot of people in this town who don't understand what it's like to be a shifter who is typically prey to larger animals." It was the rabbit shifter that spoke up once again. "All my life I have been taught to run and hide from anything that wanted to eat me. That was one of the reasons I've always felt so comfortable living in Singing Falls.

"But lately, it's not the same. There are hunters living among us. I say we go back to the old ways and just don't allow them in the community. And if that means using magic to accomplish it, then I'm all for it."

At this point the room seemed split fifty-fifty among those who agreed and those who weren't saying anything.

"And if that is to be the law, where does it end?" asked Elion. He still remained seated; his gaze locked on the witches. "What about humans? Why not take the next logical step and ban them from the community as well? After all, if we are talking threats to the supernatural community, aren't they one of the biggest? Isn't that why you constantly insist they aren't allowed to find out about us?"

Meryl stood up once again and addressed everyone. "I don't think this is a good idea. We have always been a welcoming community. Just as you said, there was a reason that you came here when you left the forest. Because you were welcomed. If we do what Jasmin is suggesting...and I have all the respect in the world for Jasmin...we could be creating a situation worse than anything we can imagine. There has to be a reason the founders never enacted this spell.

"If we do this, we are painting all wolves, all vampires, with the same brush. And they aren't all the same. No one should be singled out because of who and what they are. They deserve a chance to prove themselves, just like we all did."

Devon nodded and stood next to his wife, taking her hand. "There has to be a better way. We have wolves living among us, and if you ask me, it's made Singing Falls a better place." He turned to face Sable. "If you're not welcome in town anymore, you are welcome to stay with us. Until all of this is sorted out."

"No, she's going back to jail," said Max. "I have a brand-new cell just waiting for her."

"Over my dead body," said Elion, his voice gravelly and low.

"Buddy you're already dead," said Max. "So, taking her

back into custody shouldn't be a problem." He punctuated his statement with a slight growl.

"She hasn't done anything," replied Elion.

"She's still a suspect in the death of the librarian," answered Max.

Elion started to rise but was stopped by a clap of thunder that shook the house. Everyone looked at the witches, who seemed just as surprised.

"Wasn't us," said Jasmin.

"Alma wasn't killed by a werewolf," said a voice. It came from outside of the room and was preceded by the familiar clicking of a cane hitting Torie's hardwood floors.

Magda entered the room, her gray eyes flashing.

"What killed my sister is far more deadly than anything you could ever imagine."

Chapter Eighteen

A hushed reverence settled over the room and all eyes turned to the old witch. Everyone in her path stepped aside as she made her way forward. The ever-present Jinn walked at her side. His shirtless physique drew more than a few lingering glances.

Jasmin hurried to Magda's side, offering her arm for assistance.

"I'm old, not ancient," said Magda, brushing off Jasmin's arm.

The old witch nodded in Torie's direction and settled before them, opting to stand, her weight braced on her cane.

"Magda," said Torie, "we were not expecting you. It sounds like you have news for us."

Not one to mince words, the old witch narrowed her gaze and looked around the room. "I guess that everyone here knows about my sister by now, so there's no point in trying to keep it private. But yes, the thing that murdered her is not a werewolf."

"But we saw the body," said Jasmin. "We found evidence. Torie's magic allowed her to watch as something committed that mutilation..." She stopped, not sure how much to reveal.

"You didn't tell me that," said Magda, giving a side-eye glance to Torie.

"I...we...didn't think it was important," said Torie.

"Well, goes to show what you know," said Magda. "But that's neither here nor there. What is important is that you and the people of this town need to understand what they are dealing with. My sister was killed by a shapeshifter."

No one spoke as her words hung over the gathering like the thunderheads that seemed to always herald the old witch's arrival.

Torie frowned. "And? I mean, we knew that, right?" She looked at Jasmin for confirmation.

Magda squinted, lifting her cane off the floor only to slam it back down, loudly.

"You don't know jack," she said. "You've never met a shapeshifter. I'm not talking about a normal shifter here... I'm talking about something that is able to take the form of multiple creatures. Or humans."

That got the attention of the townsfolk who began to murmur amongst themselves before Torie held up a hand to silence them.

"I always thought shapeshifters were a myth," said Max, his deep voice low and reverential in the face of the older witch.

"Are you a myth?" snapped Magda. "If I told humans that aren't in the know about you, wouldn't they say the same thing?"

"They aren't a myth," said Elion. "But they are extremely rare. As rare as—" He looked around, his eyes settling on Leo as the little dragon seemed content with cleaning his scaly body with his tongue. "As that."

Magda stared at the vampire and nodded. "Finally. Someone who knows something."

She turned back to Torie.

"You know about were-shifters; creatures that can take the form of an animal. Well, there are other types of shifters out there that can mimic all kinds of shapes. One minute they can be a wolf. The next, a bear. The next form can be a man, and the next after that a woman. They aren't bound by any conventions of magic; all they need is physical contact with a form and then they can duplicate that form. And when I say duplicate, I mean right down to that person or creature's memories and abilities."

Torie felt a chill race up her spine. "And you are certain this is what killed Alma?"

Magda nodded. "Absolutely. I performed a magical postmortem on her myself to find out what happened."

Torie shuddered inwardly. It broke her heart to think that Magda had subjected herself to the sight of her sister's mauled body.

"Wait a minute," said Max. "How did you get to your sister's body? It's at the coroner's office, under lock and key."

Magda smiled and nodded at Jinn. "He's not just a pretty face, you know."

"If you found something other than what is in her official medical examiner's report, you'll need to share it with the M.E."

Magda made a noise deep in the back of her throat and stared the big sheriff down.

"Pssh. Your medical examiner is dead. So unless you

have a Ouija board, it's going to be a little on the hard side to share my findings with him."

Max glared at the woman and then turned his gaze to Jinn.

"What did he do?" Max said, reaching for his handcuffs.

"Oh calm down, werewolf," said Magda. "Jinn didn't do anything. He found the doctor's body shoved into one of the freezers at the place they were keeping my sister's body. That man has been dead for days."

Jasmin and Torie exchanged worried glances.

"That's not possible," Torie said. "We watched him examine Alma's body recently. We spoke with him."

The chill she felt along her spine earlier was quickly transitioning to an Arctic blast.

"Hah, if you did that, then you were talking to the shapeshifter," Magda replied. "I figured as much. That thing has been running all around town doing who knows what lately. And I'm willing to bet that the doctor wasn't the first person it's doubled. And it certainly won't be the last."

The guests were on the verge of panicking, and Torie knew it was imperative to maintain some sense of control.

"If you're right about this, then that means that Sable has nothing to do with Alma's murder. But why would Alma have been left in her room?" said Torie.

"Well, that might be true," said Magda, turning to look at Sable. "That is, as long as she isn't the shapeshifter."

Gasps rose from the townsfolk, and many of them quickly moved away from the she-wolf, trying to make their way out of the room.

"Now I'm not saying that she is," said Magda, slyly, "but I'm betting she hasn't said a word this whole time. Just sitting back and taking it in."

"And that means what?" said Jasmin. She tried to hide

it, but Torie caught the small hitch in her voice when she spoke.

"It means that I don't know you people and I have no horse in this race. Other than the fact that I'm a werewolf of course. If you don't want me in this town, that's no skin off my nose; I'll leave. I'm not keen on staying where I'm not wanted," said Sable.

Her voice was calm, and even though she spoke to the entire assemblage, her eyes were locked on Magda.

"She led the wolves to us. Why should she be allowed to stay here?" This came from someone in the group that didn't step forward. Torie made a mental note that the next time she gathered a group together like this there needed to be some sort of orderly way for people to speak. They wouldn't be allowed to just shout out any old thing when they wanted. Luckily there were not many murmurs of agreement with this.

"Because that's never been what we do," said Jasmin. "And Carl, you above all people should know that."

Whoever Carl was, Torie was glad Jasmin called him out. Hopefully that would shut him up.

"We aren't here to debate who can and cannot be in town," said Torie. "Rather, the question before the town is should we create a spell that will specifically target behavior of shifters who commit violence against the community?"

"You mean that's what we *were* here for," said Fionna. A hush settled over the crowd. "If werewolves weren't respon- sible for the murder of Alma, then maybe we need to rethink this. We have always been a peaceful community. It's obvious, due to everything that has happened over the last year, that those days may have come to an end. We aren't just a tiny community of shifters anymore. Humans are a welcome part of this town. They have been for some time now. They aren't going away. If anything, more and more of them move here every year."

"All the more reason to make Singing Falls a sanctuary," said Jasmin. "This will protect everyone who lives here."

"And what about this creature that Magda has described," said Elric. "If there is a creature out there that is capable of doing what she claims, would it be bound by the laws of your spell? What if it is a witch or another warlock that attacks the town? You can't target just us."

Torie had never heard him so heated before. Her heart ached at his words. Was he right? Is what they were doing targeting a specific subset of the supernatural community?

"He has a point, Jasmin," she said. "Would it be fair to do this based on any other criteria? We would never do it based on something like...skin tone."

Jasmin's mouth dropped open, but she didn't speak. Torie saw the hurt in her friend's eyes and immediately regretted what she said.

"I was just making a point," Torie said. "We all know nothing like that would ever happen. But what I'm saying is that what we are suggesting is tantamount to saying someone is guilty before being proven innocent. I just don't think that's how justice should work."

Jasmin nodded, her eyes hard and her voice was low and even when she spoke. "Fine. Then if everyone has had their say, why don't we put it to a vote? All those for the proposal raise your hands."

After counting those who voted for the action, she repeated the question for those who were against, and counted those hands.

"Ha!" said Magda. "It seems we have a tie." She had abstained from voting, refusing to participate in the count.

"Wait, I know how many people were here before you

came in, Magda. There was an odd number; someone is missing."

"Where is Walter?" asked Jasmin.

Torie frowned. She was pretty sure she knew which way the badger was going to vote. She looked around the room, but the badger shifter was nowhere to be seen.

He was probably back in the kitchen. She had noticed just how filled his plate was, overflowing with pizza, and he ate like someone ravenous.

"I'll check for him," said Fionna, trying to control the annoyance in her voice.

Worry clouded over Elric's face as he nodded towards Torie. "I'll check upstairs."

"I'm coming with you," said Max. "This is a big house; the two of us will be able to cover it quicker."

With that, the two wolves were off, heading out of the great room and up the staircase that led to the large loft and the guest suites.

"What was that about?" said Jasmin as she moved to stand next to Torie.

"I have no idea. Unless..."

The thought hit the two witches at the same time. They exchanged worried glances, but before either of them could say or do anything, there was a commotion at the entrance leading into the great room.

Torie looked up to see Fionna being held tightly around the neck by Walter.

"Walter, what are you doing?" Torie demanded. With a thought she summoned a flicker of magic and held it in the back of her mind. She didn't need to look over to Jasmin to see she had also drawn up her own power.

"I mean, the pizza wasn't that bad, was it?" asked

Jasmin as she slowly made her way toward the man, who tightened his grip on Fionna.

Walter smiled wickedly as he looked around the room. He could sense the magic the witches were summoning. A slight growl escaped his throat. Torie watched in horror as talons extended from his fingers and rested against Fionna's throat. She saw her friend's body stiffen in response. The badger shifter held Fionna's arm twisted behind her back in one hand and the other rested on the front of her throat.

"Either of you try anything with me, and I will rip her throat out. Trust me, as fast as you think you are, I'm faster."

Torie held her hands up slowly, palms outward, trying to calm the man down. "Walter, what is it that you want?"

"I found him in your study, Torie," said Fionna.

Walter tightened his grip on her, giving her arm a little twist. Fionna grunted in pain, and her breath caught in her throat.

"Not another word out of you," said Walter. "I'm not taking a chance on you saying some kind of trigger word the three of you might have cooked up at some point. Yes, I've done my homework, and I know how tight the three of you are."

His eyes slowly moved to the right just as Max and Elric entered the room. He backed up slowly, moving away from the two wolves.

"You two, move over there and stand with the witches where I can see you. No sudden moves or the squirrel here might just find herself without a head," said Walter.

Both of the werewolves moved slowly to stand next to Jasmin and Torie.

"What's going on here, Walter?" asked Max. "This isn't

like you. You might not be the most fun shifter to be around, but you're not a killer."

"That's because it isn't Walter," said Magda. Jinn had moved to stand in front of the old witch protectively. Both his hands were clenched into fists as he stared down the badger.

"Easy there, big guy," said Walter. "Not sure who or what you are, but you get the same warning as the wolves and these witches."

"So, you're the shapeshifter?" demanded Jasmin. "Why don't you tell us what it is that you want here?"

"I want the other part of the spell," he replied.

Torie's eyes narrowed as she realized what he was talking about. "You. You're the one who killed Alma, aren't you? You're the one who stole those pages from the grimoire."

Walter gave a savage smile and focused his attention on Torie. "Can't get anything past you, huh? All I need is the part of the spell you and your friend have hidden somewhere. I have the reversal part, now I need the activation spell."

"Even if you have it, it won't do you any good," said Jasmin. "You're not a witch, you can't cast the spell."

"Who said it was for me?" said Walter smugly.

"Doesn't matter," said Jasmin. She reached up with her forefinger and tapped the side of her head. "The spell is in here. We burned the hard copy."

Walter responded with a growl and then a low chuckle.

"You're lying," he said. "I know the spell was hidden in the original document that was created when this town was founded. That is a priceless artifact, so there is no way you would destroy it." He turned his attention to Magda and offered her his salacious smile. "It would be spitting on the memory of your sister to destroy something like that."

Magda's gray eyes sparked dangerously. "Wrong thing to say, monster," she said.

Torie could see the old witch's lips moving in silent invocation of a spell. In the distance, thunder rumbled, growing louder with each passing second. Walter's body stiffened in response as he looked around the room.

"Whatever you're doing, stop. I promise you I will kill this bi—"

Before he could complete the threat, a bolt of lightning shattered the window and struck him in the back. He howled, letting go of Fionna as his body contorted in pain.

Fionna threw herself across the room and away from the killer just as Torie and Jasmin advanced on him. Both had circles of magical power glowing around their hands as they prepared to attack.

In a flash, Walter shifted into the form of a huge black leopard and roared in defiance at the women.

Torie struck first, firing a bolt of magic at the beast, only to have it miss as he leapt into the air, shifting into the form of a hawk. In the blink of an eye, Elric shifted into his hybrid wolf form and leapt at the bird, wrapping his powerful arms around it as they both crashed to the floor.

Walter shifted again, this time becoming a large red wolf. He turned, latching onto Elric's shoulder with his massive jaws and biting down hard enough to make him howl. He twisted, throwing the werewolf off him and towards Jasmin, who was circling around for her own attack.

Walter saw Max draw his revolver from its holster and try to get a bead on him. He moved fast, leaping into the screaming group of people who stood transfixed by the sudden display of violence among them.

Max instantly lifted his gun away from the crowd, breathing curses as he tried to get a bead on where Walter had run to. The crowd parted, but Walter was nowhere to be seen.

"Where did he go?" shouted Max.

"There!" It was Elion who spoke up. He pointed to the floor in the corner of the room.

A large viper was coiled on the floor, hissing at them. It focused its attention on Magda and struck with blinding speed at the old witch.

Magda could only close her eyes and instinctively brought up an arm to try and ward off the bite she knew was coming.

It was a bite that never reached her.

She opened her eyes to see the giant snake being held fast in Jinn's grip. The big elf held the snake with both hands as he began to apply pressure, intent on choking the beast.

Before he could complete the kill, Walter shifted yet again. This time, his form became that of a large bear, one that raised a clawed hand overhead, ready to bring it slashing down on the shirtless elf.

"That will be enough out of you," said Elion as he raced forward to grab the large grizzly from behind. His speed and strength were too much for the shifter. Elion lifted the beast off the ground.

"Elion, don't kill it!" said Jasmin. "We need questions answered."

Just then, Walter shifted one last time, returning to his hawk form. The sudden change in form allowed him to slip free of Elion's grasp. Once freed, Walter made for the broken window and flew out. He was gone, slipping away into the night sky before anyone could attempt to follow him.

Chapter Nineteen

Although it was not needed, Torie found herself apologizing profusely to her friends and guests as she thanked them for coming. She was thankful no one had been seriously hurt in the melee and promised everyone she would host another get together soon to make it up to them. Understandably, not many of the townsfolk seemed overly enthusiastic at the prospect.

Meryl and Devon were the last to leave, and they gave both Jasmin and Torie a quick hug on their way out the door.

"No matter what happened here tonight, just know this is not indicative of all shifter behavior. Stay true to who you are; don't give into fear," Meryl said, squeezing both of their hands as she walked out the door.

Once everyone was gone, Torie joined her friends in the great room. She walked slowly over to the shattered window, being careful to avoid the glass. Letting out a deep sigh, she turned her attention to the few who remained in the room.

Fionna had left almost immediately, refusing any

medical care, and saying that all she wanted was to get home to Glen. Jasmin had made her promise to have Glen check her out before she would agree to her leaving.

Max walked over to Torie, bits of glass crunching under his heavy boots.

"Really?" said Torie. "You're just going to track glass throughout the house. Watch where you're stepping."

"I'm sorry. I wasn't thinking. I just wanted to say that I need to go. I should swing by Walter's place, see if he's there."

"Why bother? He's dead, I can assure you." It was Magda who spoke up. She sat at the far side of the room in a wing-back chair. Jinn stood silently next to her. "Anytime that shifter doubles someone or something, the original dies."

"Yeah, well, maybe you don't know everything," said Max.

"Never said I did," she replied. "But go on...look for him and let us know what you find."

Max turned to leave the room but was stopped by Torie's hand on his arm.

"Max, wait, there's something we need to talk about."

She walked over to the sofa opposite from where Magda sat, and motioned for Max and Elric to join her. As soon as she sat down, Leo jumped onto her lap. The little dragon had been understandably anxious and clingy since the attack.

It was his first exposure to a large group of people, and Torie was afraid it might have traumatized the little fella. She stroked him reassuringly as she waited for everyone to be seated.

Elion and Sable moved closer but declined the invitation to sit.

Max looked at Torie expectantly. "Well, what is so important?"

"Why are you being such an ass, Max?" asked Jasmin.

"Oh, I don't know. Maybe it's because my bloodthirsty brother is out there plotting my takedown without giving a crap about what happens to the people who get in his way."

That was when Torie realized what Max was going through. He, the big strong alpha male, was afraid. Not afraid for himself, but rather he was afraid for those he had come to care for. Including every member of this town that had adopted him as their protector.

"Max, that's what I want to talk to you about," Torie said, her voice soft and controlled to reduce the anxiety radiating off him. "Did that wolf look familiar to you?"

"What wolf?" he asked.

"The one the shifter turned into during the fight. I could swear that is the same wolf we fought up on the ridge. The one that got away."

Max furrowed his brow, scratching at his chin as he thought back to the battle.

"It...could have been. It looked like the same wolf. But how can that be? I caught its scent. It definitely smelled like a member of the Idle Winds pack."

Torie considered what he said, then turned to Magda.

"Didn't you say this shapeshifter could mimic any one they came into contact with? Down to their abilities even? Would that extend to the way they smell; to a degree that it could fool a werewolf?"

The old witch considered the question and slowly nodded her head.

"I suppose it would be possible. In many ways, the shapeshifter becomes the person or being they double. Now, there may be limitations to that. Would they be able to duplicate the more esoteric nature of a vampire, let's say? I wouldn't know."

"So there's no way they could double a witch and have our powers, correct?" asked Jasmin.

"That I would say would be beyond their abilities," replied Magda. "Physical characteristics are one thing, but they cannot manipulate mystical energy the way we can. Even if they were learning incantations, they could not cast a spell because they are not connected to the lore which we are born to."

"So, they can grow vampire fangs and drink blood, but they can't cast fireballs if they were to double Torie?"

"That's correct. If they were to double Torie, it would be in looks only."

"Is there a way to spot them? I mean, they were here the entire night, and we had no idea," said Torie.

"Not only were they in your house, but they had free range in your home," said Magda. "The girl it held hostage said it was in your private study. What do you keep in there?"

"Nothing out of the ordinary. Maybe a few personal bits of paper, some keepsakes perhaps. Mostly just my books and some things from my mother."

"And this document they were looking for? I take it you didn't burn it," said Magda.

"Of course not," said Jasmin. "I have it safe and secure at my house. It's under lock and ward, so no one will be getting to it."

"All of this is fine and well," said Max, "but how does it help us to stop my brother?"

"I think this is all related somehow," replied Torie. "Why else would the shapeshifter have infiltrated your brother's pack? Why would it have then been here trying to steal the original founders' document that has part of the spell needed for turning Singing Falls into a sanctuary? There has to be a connection. We just aren't seeing it."

"I think the question is, what does this shifter want?" said Elion.

It was the first time the vampire had spoken, and all eyes turned to him.

"Maybe to distract us," said Torie. "I think we are drifting further away from our initial goal here."

"And what was that?" asked Magda.

"To find a way to break the fated bond between two wolves," said Torie. "Sable and Elric are fated mates. But Elric is with me now, and Sable is with Elion. But the bond between them…"

Magda's eyes widened at the revelation. "You weren't seriously going to attempt to do that, were you?"

Not a word was spoken as everyone's eyes darted back and forth between them.

"That bond is sacred," said Magda. "Chosen by the fates and bestowed on certain supernaturals. Trying to undo it would be like…trying to change the tides."

The witch's words caused Elion to chuckle. "You witches and your penchant for drama. Of course the bond can be broken. It was created by magic so magic can break it."

"I didn't say it couldn't be done. But doing it will have a lot of far-reaching ramifications." said Magda.

"Well, we need to bring this back around to figuring out how to do that," said Torie. "If we can do that, it might help us defuse this situation with Max's brother."

"And figure out what the shifter has to do with all of this," added Elion.

Torie looked over at Jasmin, who had remained silent

during the last exchange. Her friend was looking at her intently, her lips pursed. Torie could sense she was disappointed but wasn't about to open the floor back up to discussion.

"That shifter is far more dangerous than even I thought," said Magda. "It will do you well to track that thing down and put an end to it before it kills more people."

"What do you know, Magda?" asked Jasmin. Something in the old witch's voice caught her attention. "You know something, don't you? Spill it."

Magda looked around, her eyes flashing in the light. "I was able to discern certain characteristics about the shifter when we fought. Namely, there is a duality to their presence that might explain why they are so interested in the spells the two of you, and my sister, stumbled across."

"What do you mean, duality?" asked Jasmin.

"That creature is a chimera," replied Magda.

Torie noticed a slight shiver run through Elion as he leaned forward. "A chimera? Are you certain? Interesting…"

"Isn't a chimera a fire-breathing creature that is part lion, part goat, part woman? Or something like that?" asked Torie.

"In ancient mythology, yes. But that isn't the kind of chimera we are dealing with. You forget that in the supernatural, there are crossroads where magic and science intersect," said Magda. "In the world of science, a chimera is a single organism that is made up of two different types of DNA."

"Wait, how is that possible?" asked Torie.

"Typically, it happens when a fetus absorbs its twin. The two can fuse into one," said Magda.

"It also happens when people undergo bone marrow

transplants. Their marrow is killed off and replaced with that of a donor. It triggers the growth of new red blood cells, with those cells being from the donor. Two DNA strands in one," said Elion.

Jasmin made a face at the vampire. "Do I even want to know how you know that?"

"Probably not," he admitted.

She looked away, turning to face Magda. "But more importantly, how do you know all of this about that shifter?"

"I was able to glean a lot of information from it when I struck it with that lightning bolt."

"So, you weren't trying to kill?" said Torie.

"Oh heavens no. Although I'm not entirely sure a full-powered bolt would have done it, judging from what I was able to see. I am an elemental witch; I can manipulate the four elements, and lightning is just a combination of fire and wind for me."

"But how did that tell you what was going on inside the creature?" asked Jasmin.

"Well, you gather information through spells and incantation. For me, I can do the same thing with my elements. When I struck the shifter, it was a two-way attack. The lightning collected information and sent it back to me. That was when I realized there were definitely two different personalities inside."

"Is that normal for a chimera?" asked Torie.

"Absolutely not. Most people never know they are a chimera unless they have to undergo genetic testing for some reason," said Magda. "But here again, magic and science have intersected. In the case of a supernatural chimera, the one who was absorbed, possesses a fully formed consciousness."

"Oh my God," said Torie. "That sounds terrible."

"I didn't get the impression that it was," said Magda. "They weren't fighting; there was no single personality that was dominant. It was more like they were a team; two minds, perfectly in control of one body. But that's not all. There was a lot of magical knowledge locked in there as well. One of them was actively preparing counter-spells to deal with whatever Torie and Jasmin might have thrown at them."

"This is just getting weirder and weirder," said Jasmin. "Could this all be a result of someone the shifter doubled and then killed? Maybe a psychic straggler of some kind?"

"Interesting theory," said Magda. "It's possible; but like I said, that would not explain the knowledge of the mystic arts I saw, or their ability to command magic. No, this is so entwined in the shifter that it has to have been there since birth."

"But why would it be involved with my brother and his pack? There is nothing they have that would interest a creature like this," said Max.

"Possibly," added Magda. "I'm betting that you figure that out, then everything else will fall into place."

"Well, I'm tired of waiting," said Max, getting to his feet. "If Arin is in town, or just outside it, I'll find him the old-fashioned way." He looked at Elric, giving his old beta a long stare.

"I'm joining him," said Elric.

"You guys, please," said Torie. "This town can't take an all-out brawl. To say nothing of the fact that you are probably outnumbered."

"We're going as well. I can help even the odds," said Elion. He stood, taking Sable's hand in his.

"I'm sorry for this," said Sable. "But this is wolf business. I had hoped to end this quietly. Hoped that you could sever the bond between myself and Elric, but I don't know if we have time to wait for that any longer."

It wasn't in her nature to argue against so many, but Torie could feel the urge bubbling up from deep within. She looked to Jasmin for support only to have her friend avert her eyes.

Torie huffed. It was all she could do to keep from saying, 'et-tu, Brute'. Magda eyed the two of them but kept quiet as well.

There was a loud chirping coming from Jasmin's pocket, and she fished out her phone, eying the screen before placing it against her ear.

"Hey there, what's up—" She cut her words short as her face scrunched into a mask of concern before her eyes widened in disbelief. "Don't move, we're on our way."

"What is it?" said Torie, getting to her feet.

"That was Glen. A shifter just broke into their house and took Fionna."

Chapter Twenty

For Most, recovering from being knocked unconsciousness was like swimming up from the bottom of a lake filled with thick, dark oil.

But Fionna wasn't just anyone. Her shifter sense of hearing and awareness came around first, and she instinctively knew not to move. She could tell she was in a horizontal position, her hands and feet restrained. She resisted the urge to open her eyes and look around. Instead, she listened, allowing her other senses to feel out the space in which she was contained.

Her nose told her she was underground. The smell of earth and moss was incredibly strong, more so than it was above ground. There was also the scent of fresh limestone and clay. She focused on her hearing and picked up the distant sound of water dripping slowly into a pool. She could not pick up any running water, however, so she wasn't near a stream or river.

When she didn't hear voices, she stuck just the tip of her tongue between her lips to taste the air. It was acrid and salty at the same time. Like licking a salt block covered in volcanic ash.

Where was she? What had happened to her?

She remembered being at home with Glen, who was looking at the bruises on her neck where that shifter had held her in a death grip. Her throat had been so sore; it was hard to swallow, and her tongue felt a little swollen inside her mouth. Glen had offered to make her some tea with honey to help assuage the pain.

And then what...?

There was a crash that came from somewhere in the back of the house. Something rushed into the kitchen where they were sitting...something that moved incredibly fast. It lunged at Fionna, grabbing her once again in that steel-hard grip. Glen had leapt at it, trying to get it off of Fionna, but the creature was way too fast and strong. The last thing Fionna remembered was Glen being swatted across the kitchen.

Then there was blackness that crept into the corners of her vision, and everything switched off. Until now.

Growing up as a squirrel shifter, learning to rely on her senses had saved her life more times than she could count. Her senses were highly attuned to the presence of others; especially if those others were a threat to her. It had almost become a sixth sense for her; and right now, it was telling her she wasn't alone.

"Well, you might as well open your eyes, little shifter." The voice seemed to be coming from everywhere around her. "I know you're awake. And you know I'm here watching you, so why don't we both just cut the charades?"

Fionna frowned slightly and made a show of recovering consciousness. She feigned more pain than she felt and slowly began to roll her head from side to side to add to her confused look. Her mind was racing as she tried to figure out next steps.

Flexing her arms, she tested the strength of the binds that held her. Instantly she felt red-hot pain sear through her wrists.

"Oh, I wouldn't pull too hard. There are barbs imbedded in your flesh attached to those chains. It's to prevent you from shifting to your smaller form and trying to scamper off. You shift and those hooks in you will probably pull your little hands right off. Do you think a shifter could heal from an injury like that?"

Fionna huffed and craned her head around, trying to locate the source of the voice. Finally, she saw a shadow detach itself from the wall to her left and make its way slowly towards her.

Wherever she was being held, it was dimly lit, and she could just make out rough, earthen walls all around her. The rock ceiling was low as well, and she could make out small, iron hooks that had been driven into it at various intervals. Hanging from one of the hooks was a gas lantern.

At least now she knew the source of the light and she felt even more certain that she was in a cave of some kind. Not that that information would have helped her; she knew that much of the mountainous region around Singing Falls was littered with cave systems. Many of which had never been explored. But there was something different about this one; it was enclosed in the earth, but it felt more manmade.

And something about it seemed familiar to the shifter.

Fionna blinked away cobwebs and focused on the face leaning over her. It was definitely the shifter from Torie's party who had grabbed her; there was no doubt about that. But the face sneering down at her was that of someone she knew only too well, and there was no way it belonged to the shifter.

Fionna was looking up into the eyes of Alma, her first true love.

"Do you like it?" asked the shifter. "I picked this one because I could see your face in her mind's eye when I killed her and took her form. I thought maybe you'd like to see her one last time."

Fionna struggled against her binds, dismissing the pain that fired through her with every move.

"Monster! I will kill you for this!" she spat.

"Even if you were free, I don't think that would be possible," the shifter said. "But I didn't bring you here to fight."

"Whatever you want, I'm not doing it," Fionna said.

The shifter walked slowly away, trailing a single finger along Fionna's arm in a way that made her flesh crawl.

"Poor little shifter. You think you have a choice in the matter?" Fionna struggled again, testing the chains that rattled every time she moved. "Please stop doing that. You're going to hurt yourself, and I need you whole."

"Where am I?" Fionna asked. "And what did you do with Glen? I swear if you've hurt her I will—"

"You mean your girlfriend? The one you replaced me with? You hurt my feelings with that, you know?"

The fake Alma leaned over Fionna once again, this time, her face was slack, and a single tear dropped from one eye. Even though Fionna knew it wasn't her, the visual struck her in the stomach just as hard as if the shifter had physically punched her.

"Yes, see when I took this form, I gained her memories as well. That's how I knew who had the spell I need. Your friend Jasmin has it. But I don't know what they did with it.

I thought maybe they had it at the little town gathering Torie hosted...but no. It wasn't there."

"Why do you want a spell? You aren't a witch. It will do you no good," said Fionna.

The shifter caressed Fionna's face lightly. "Don't you worry your pretty little head about that. I just need you because I need something to offer the witches as a trade for the spell. And something tells me, you're the one thing they would barter for."

Fionna jerked her face away from the shifter's hand. "No, they won't. You've shown your hand, and they will do whatever it takes to stop you. You're as good as dead, you know that?"

The shifter laughed and stepped back. "They got lucky back at the house. I wasn't expecting the vampire to be as strong as he was. But I have a plan for him and the were-wolves as well. They will be so busy they won't have time to get involved in our little exchange."

"You don't know them the way I do. They won't help you. And I certainly won't."

"Oh, you're right about that," the shifter said.

Fionna sensed a ripple of magic flow through the air, and this time, when the shifter leaned over her, she was staring at a new face.

"But here's the thing, darling. You've already helped me."

Shock flowed through Fionna's system as she looked up into her own eyes. She watched in horror as a mirror image of herself lifted a rock and brought it crashing down on the side of her head, sending her once more into blackness's tight embrace.

Chapter Twenty-One

Glen was understandably inconsolable. Even as Torie tried to hold an iceberg to the large knot forming on her forehead, she was only concerned for her wife.

"No, forget about me," she said, pushing the bag away. "Please, you have to go after Fionna. That thing has her, and who knows what it's doing to her!"

"Glen, we are going to get her back, don't even worry about that," said Jasmin. "But you need to get this looked at. There's an ambulance on the way, and we will be able to focus on getting Fionna back if we know you're going to be alright. So, promise you'll let them treat you?"

"Yes, of course," said Glen, sinking back against the couch.

"Glen, did the shifter that attacked you say anything that stood out? Anything that could give us a clue as to where they might have gone?" asked Torie.

Glen thought, but finally shook her head in despair. "No, nothing. I'm sorry, it all happened so fast. It was a blur..."

"We might have something," said Max.

He and Elric were outside, examining where the breach into the house had occurred.

"There is a scent here, on the grounds just outside the windows. Definitely a wolf. One from the Idle Winds pack."

Torie turned to Glen. "Could you tell if there was just one attacker or multiple?"

Glen's brow furrowed. "I'm sure it was just one. It came through the window, and...I don't remember there being anyone else."

Elric nodded at Torie. "There are multiple prints and scents here. At least three others were present."

"But that doesn't mean they took Fionna," said Torie. "The shifter was alone at the house, why now surround itself with werewolves?"

"It wasn't alone when it attacked us on the ridge," said Max. "Maybe my brother is trying to send me another message. He's trying to draw me out again."

Elric was nodding. "Yes, that would make sense. He's been playing us all along and now wants to end things."

"Good," said Max, "because so do I. Let's follow the trail and end this."

"What is going on here?" questioned Torie. "This isn't like the two of you. Think this through."

Elric's eyes glowed yellow as he regarded the witches. "I think we've been thinking too much. It's time to act." He turned his back to Torie and signaled to Max. "I'll call Sable and tell her and Elion to meet us. It's time to end this game once and for all."

They turned to leave, but Torie reached out to grasp Elric by his shirt sleeve.

"Elric, wait," she said. "This doesn't feel right."

He turned and held her at arm's length. "I don't want

you hurt, Torie. I need you to stay out of this; sit this one out. Max, Sable and I will handle this. Between us and Elion, we are more than capable of doing whatever needs to be done."

Before she could counter, the two werewolves were out of the house, shifting into their nimbler forms as they sprinted down the drive and away from the house.

"I don't get it," said Jasmin. Her voice was tinged with anger. "What has gotten into them? It can't just be pack mentality doing this."

Torie swallowed hard and turned to her friend. "Jasmin, I have to tell you something. Something I probably should have mentioned well before now, but I didn't think it was really that important at the time."

Jasmin cocked her head to one side and looked at her friend. "Torie. What did you do?"

She told Jasmin about the spell she attempted to cast and how nothing had happened as a result. Once she was finished, Jasmin glared at her as she struggled to control her breathing and calm her beating heart.

"I know, I know," said Torie. "Not one of my brighter moves. I just...I was afraid of losing him; I had to try something."

Jasmin's stern look softened a bit but then returned to granite as she shook her head at her friend.

"When this is over, we are having a very long conversation about self-worth; do you hear me?" she said.

Torie felt her cheeks burn at the admonition. Of course Jasmin was right, and she knew it; why the hell had she been so scared over the thought of a man leaving her? When had she become so desperate to be with someone that she was willing to resort to magic to hold onto them?

Jasmin eased up a bit on her and took her by the hand.

"We can deal with whatever is going on inside that head of yours later. Right now, we need to focus on saving Fionna. It's just me and you, so we have to be on the same page."

Torie had not heard truer words spoken in days. There had been a divide between them, one that was making each doubt the other. Of course, what Torie had done didn't go very far in helping to ease those doubts, but coming clean had felt like a huge first step.

She nodded. No matter what was going on between them, they were still a united front.

A formidable front, Torie thought, as the shifter was going to find out.

"How do we find her?" asked Torie.

"Locator spell. We get a personal artifact of Fionna's from Glen and use it to track her. I'm betting wherever she is, we find the shifter that grabbed her."

"And we make that creature sorry they ever set foot in Singing Falls," said Torie. Her voice and resolve were steel at this point.

They turned to find Glen and were met with a terrified scream from the woman. She was standing at the sink in the counter, her eyes glued to the sliding doors that led to the patio.

Standing in the frame of the open doors was Fionna. Blood flowed freely down her face, covering her top as she tried to balance herself against the door siding. There was a pool of blood pooling at her feet. It was coming from her arm.

Or what was left of the arm. It had been torn away just below the elbow.

Fionna had tied her belt around the stump and was looking at her wife with pleading, nearly vacant eyes. She reached out with her good hand, tried to speak, and collapsed onto the kitchen floor.

The pain shooting through her body brought her back into consciousness. Torie and Glen had placed her on the dining room table and were working frantically to save her life.

"She's lost so much blood," Glen was saying. "We need to get her to the hospital now!"

"I agree," said Torie. "What happened to her...her arm is...this doesn't even look like a clean cut..."

There was a slamming of the front door as Jasmin rushed back into the room.

"I've got my car backed up to the porch. We can load her into the back and head for the hospital."

"No...no hospital...no time for that," Fionna muttered through chattering teeth.

"Baby, you are going to die if we don't—" started Glen.

Fionna shook her head. "No, I won't. Just need...just need to stop the bleeding. Please."

"How," said Torie, looking around frantically. "What do we do?" She looked at Glen, who had slipped into shock seeing her wife in the condition she was in. Torie grabbed her around the shoulders and shook the woman. "Glen! How do we stop the bleeding?"

Glen blinked rapidly, shaking herself out of her despair.

"Heat. Fire! We can cauterize the stump!"

Jasmin and Torie looked at one another, each thinking the same thing. Jasmin moved to the head of the table and placed both hands around Fionna's head, staring deeply into her eyes. Torie moved to stand next to her mangled arm.

"Fionna, this is going to hurt," Jasmin said. "I'm going to mitigate that as much as possible, okay?"

Fionna nodded, trying to force a smile. "Do it."

Jasmin concentrated, pouring her hex power into her hands; the soft white light began to pulse, suffusing Fionna in magic. Closing her eyes, Jasmin began to chant.

"Moon that's full, or moon that wanes,
help this woman, endure the pain."

She repeated the enchantment over and over, each time focusing deeper into Fionna until she felt the squirrel shifter was ready. Then she nodded at Torie.

Torie closed her eyes and whispered silently to herself. When she opened them, they glowed bright with power. Power that she then channeled into her hands until a ball of bright orange fire glowed between them. Then, before her own resolve could falter, she shoved the fire onto Fionna's bloodied arm.

Even with Jasmin's power flowing through her, Fionna screamed. Her body contorted in agony as the flesh of her limb was seared; muscle, tissue and bone fused into a single closed mass of charred meat.

Glen cried out as well, turning away from them, unable to bear the agony that her wife was enduring. When it was over, she turned, wiping away her tears, and rushed to her wife's side. To her surprise, Fionna was awake, her eyes focusing on her friends.

"Okay. Remind me to never go through that again," she said, her voice raspy and pain-filled.

"Oh my God...Fionna," said Glen, bending over to hug her wife and cover her head with kisses. "Are you okay?"

Fionna tried to force a smile. "No, I'm not okay...I just

got my torn off arm melted." She saw the look of horror on Glen's face and immediately regretted the bad joke. "Hey, it's okay. I'm going to be okay. We shifters can heal from almost anything that doesn't kill us. I'll be good as new in a couple of months."

Glen looked at Jasmin and Torie hopefully.

Jasmin nodded. "I mean, Max got his eye ripped out and I swear it's slowly growing back. So, maybe?"

"When I'm a little stronger, I'll shift back into my squirrel form," said Fionna. "We heal faster in our animal forms. I just...I need to sleep for a bit is all."

Torie cleared her throat. "Yes, you do that. You rest as long as you want. But...and I hate to ask this...can you tell us anything about what happened?"

Fionna frowned and exhaled sharply, grimacing at the ache in her arm. Even with Jasmin's magic flowing through her, the pain was considerable.

"That shifter...it had me. Took me to one of the old salt mines outside of town. I knew that place seemed familiar. It's where I used to play as a kid with some of the other shifters in the woods. We were not supposed to go into them, but it was the best place to play hide and seek."

She started coughing, the effort turning her face into a mask of agony. Glen reached for her, intent on stopping the interrogation, but Fionna motioned that she wanted to continue.

"She had me in some weird, barbaric trap that she thought would keep me from shifting. But joke's on her," she lifted her amputated arm at them. "I chewed through my arm."

Torie clasped a hand over her mouth, her eyes filling with tears for her friend. "God almighty. Did she say anything to you? What did it want?"

"It wants the first part of the spell. The one it says Jasmin has. It said I was the weak link, and it was going to use me to force you to hand it over…but then…something happened. It wasn't alone in the mine. It struck me in the head with a rock just as someone came into the cave. I wasn't completely out; I could just make out what was said."

"What did they say?" asked Jasmin.

"It said, 'so that's where it is', and then they left in a hurry," replied Fionna. "She knows where you put it."

Jasmin looked up in horror. "Oh no. I gave it to Magda for safe keeping rather than leave it at my house unguarded! Torie, we have to get to her."

As soon as she spoke the words, Fionna's head snapped up and she smiled. Only it wasn't the warm, loving smile they had grown to know from their friend. Instead, it was a dark, menacing grin. The way a skull would look if someone tried stretching skin across it, exposing only the teeth.

Taking advantage of the shock around her, Fionna leapt off the table, a sneer on her face.

"Thanks. Should have known you'd leave it with that old bat. Thanks for the info."

She backed away from them, holding up her mangled arm as she began to shift forms.

"Hey, boys, come on in! I got what I need."

There was a shattering of glass as the sliding doors imploded. The picture window at the front of the house shattered as two enormous wolves leapt into the house. They snarled and shook glass from their hides, saliva dripping from their maws as they advanced on the witches.

The shifter shed her clothes as her body transformed into that of a huge hawk, lifting off the ground and heading for the broken windows.

"Kill them all. I'll deal with the old one." And with that, the creature they had mistaken for their friend set off into the night sky.

Jasmin turned to Torie, shock and confusion on her face, just as the first wolf, all claws and fangs, leapt at them.

Chapter Twenty-Two

Jasmin threw a shield up before the wolf could shred the two witches. Striking the barrier, the werewolf bounced off, crashing to the floor. Rising to its hind legs, it lashed out, raking the glowing force field with claws, causing sparks of light to fly from the barrier.

Torie focused her magic, calling on the same fire she had recently used to heal the deceptive shifter.

"Now!" she called.

Jasmin mentally opened a small hole at the front of her shield and Torie shoved her hands at it, throwing a blast of fire at the raging beast. It howled in response, throwing itself to one side to avoid taking the full brunt of the blast.

Torie turned to see the second wolf stalking up behind them, its yellow eyes searching for any weakness in Jasmin's shields. Behind the wolf, a large bookshelf was anchored to the wall, and opposite that a massive flat-screen television sat on a media stand.

"TV!" Torie shouted, pointing at the screen and then

the wolf. Her magic pulled the television from the stand and sent it flying in the wolf's direction.

The creature leapt deftly to the side, out of the path of the object that hurtled its way. Torie smiled. That was exactly what she hoped it would do.

"Bookcase!" she yelled, just as the wolf landed from dodging the television. The werewolf did not have time to adjust and found itself crushed beneath the weight of the towering case that landed in a crash on top of it.

She knew it wasn't dead, but hopefully it would be stunned long enough for the two of them to deal with the first wolf.

It had circled around, snarling at the pain the witches had inflicted upon it. Half of its body had been burned, the hair and flesh singed almost completely off by Torie's fire. It roared in pain and charged at them.

Jasmin dropped her shields completely as Torie summoned a dagger of pure magic and flung it at the beast, striking it in the side. The wolf was prepared for their attack, and moving faster than they could follow, it rolled out of the line of her mystic attack.

Coming to its feet, it shifted into a hybrid man-wolf form and used razor-sharp, powerful talons to dig into the flooring. With a powerful heave, it hurled a chunk of wood and sub flooring at the witches. Jasmin barely had time to get her shields back up so that the incoming projectile struck it and not them. There was a spray of sparks, splinters and dust that momentarily blinded the witches.

Jasmin was stunned by the impact, and her shield flickered briefly around them. That was the only opening the wolf needed.

In a flash, it reverted to full wolf and pounced, jaws open and ready to snap tight on their flesh.

A boom so loud it nearly deafened everyone in the house rang out, and the wolf's head exploded in a shower of red and white.

Torie looked around bewildered, only to see Glen standing behind where the wolf had just been with her shotgun still pointed at the red mist swirling in the air.

"Huh, so much for needing silver," she said. Then her eyes grew wide. "Get down!" she yelled as she brought her gun up once more and pointed it at the witches.

Instinctively, Torie and Jasmin dropped to the ground just as the second wolf reappeared after having dug itself out from under the bookcase. Glen fired her gun, emptying the second shell, but the wolf was too fast. It leapt to the side, badly grazed by the gunfire. This time, it altered its target, moving away from the witches to bear down on Glen.

The woman screamed and turned the shotgun around, so that she held it by the barrel like a baseball bat. She knew it wouldn't do much against the massive beast that had zeroed in on her, but there was no way she was going down without a fight.

An instant before the wolf made contact, something entered the room, moving equally as fast as the werewolf. It slammed into the monster, knocking it onto its side.

Then, before the stunned women could react, Elric was on top of the beast, locking both arms around its neck.

He pulled up and back with all his strength and was rewarded with the popping and cracking sound of the beast's neck breaking. He took a deep breath, shifted from hybrid back to his human form and looked at the women.

"You just love throwing these parties without me, huh?" he said.

Torie rushed to him, engulfing him in a bear hug.

"What are you doing here? You're supposed to be helping Max," she said.

Elric smiled. "I don't know. Something just didn't feel right. I rushed out of here to go with him, but part of me knew you were right. We were moving way too fast and not stopping to think. He has Elion and Sable. They can face his brother if it comes down to it. But I belong at your side; now and forever."

He lowered his head to kiss her and only lifted it back up when Jasmin started making fake gagging noises.

"Thank you for the save, Elric. But we had this," she said, nodding at Glen.

For her part, Glen was still a wreck, her face a ghastly pale shade that placed her one step above passing out.

"Where is Fionna? What was that...that thing, that was pretending to be her?"

Torie and Jasmin exchanged worried glances, each afraid to voice what they were both thinking.

"Glen, I want you to reload your gun and barricade yourself in one of the back bedrooms, okay?" said Torie. "You don't come out until we come back for you, understand?"

As if in a dream, Glen nodded and shuffled off to do as she was told. Then she stopped and turned to face them.

"How will I know if it's you and not that thing pretending to be you?"

Torie paused. "Because the thing won't be in any condition to double anyone else once we are finished with it. And we are going to bring Fionna back as well."

Glen shambled off to the back of the house, and Torie looked over to see Jasmin staring at her, eyes moist as she swallowed the lump in her throat.

"Torie, you know what that means if the shifter was imitating Fionna, right? She's—"

Torie cut her off before she could finish her sentence. "No. She isn't. She can't be."

She rushed over to the table where the shifter had been lying and turned to Elric.

"Can you get any kind of scent off this? Is there any way you can follow it back to wherever it came from? I'm betting that is where the shifter was holding Fionna. Find her. Bring her back to us, no matter what you have to do."

There was an edge to her voice that neither Jasmin nor Elric had heard before. The big wolf nodded his head and shifted. He approached the table on all fours, taking long sniffs across the top of it and all around the base. Then, without looking back, he bolted out of the house and disappeared into the woods.

"And us?" said Jasmin, already knowing what the response would be.

"We need to get to Magda. Fast. If that shifter is there, I'm betting it isn't alone. There were two wolves here, who knows how many others might be working with it."

"They have to be from Max's brother's pack. Why would they be helping a shapeshifter?"

"We'll worry about that when the time comes. Right now, we need to get to Magda."

Torie held out her hands, and Jasmin took them in hers. Together, they chanted.

"Merciful spirits we call to thee,
deliver us to where we need to be."

In a swirl of light, and a blast of power, the two witches

vanished, as the power of their combined hex carried them from one chaotic moment in space, to a potentially far worse one.

Chapter Twenty-Three

They reappeared in a patch of woods just outside Magda's cottage. Torie dropped to one knee, her body fighting the disorientation and vertigo that accompanied using their hex power to teleport over distances.

"You okay?" asked Jasmin, rubbing her friend's back.

"I will be, just need to catch my breath." She closed her eyes and focused on a few deep breaths to center herself.

"Well, that's good to hear. Because there's a wolf staring at us."

Torie felt the air crackle as Jasmin summoned magic and channeled it into her fists. Looking up, Torie saw the werewolf watching them from about fifteen feet away. A distance that could have been covered in a single leap from the beast.

So why were they still alive?

She felt the tension flow through Jasmin's body as she prepared to launch an attack at the wolf. That was when she grabbed her arm.

"Jasmin, wait. I know that wolf."

As if on cue, the large wolf walked out of the brush, silently padding up to the witches.

"Max," said Torie, "what are you doing here?"

His voice began to flow into Torie's mind as he began speaking, but Torie quickly shook her head.

"No, Max. My particular hex power allows me to hear you in your wolf form, but Jasmin can't. She needs to hear this as well."

Max shifted back to human and started over.

"My apologies," he nodded to Jasmin, "I didn't realize you don't all have the same abilities. As I said, I was tracking Arin; his scent led me to this place. It goes cold at the entrance to that house. What are you doing here?"

"Your brother is in there?" asked Jasmin, her brow furrowing. "That's Magda's house."

"Long story short, the shapeshifter tricked us into revealing that Magda has the original founding documents that contain the hex spell. We came here hoping to surprise the shifter and take it out."

"Where is Elric?" Max said. "He went back for you."

"He's rescuing Fionna. We hope," said Jasmin, throwing a worried look at Torie.

"Where are Sable and Elion?" asked Torie.

"They're watching from the other side of the house. We were going to move on them, but then you two showed up."

"Do you have any idea what's going on in there?" asked Jasmin.

The wolf shook his head. "We can't hear anything inside the house. But we can smell a lot of magic brewing."

Torie reached out with her senses and nodded, confirming what Max had said.

"Yeah, the house is warded. No wonder even their senses can't penetrate it," she said.

"This is not good," said Jasmin, looking upward at the sky. "It's too quiet. No thunder rumbling."

Torie nodded as understanding dawned on her. "Magda isn't using her powers to defend herself."

"So either she's dead..." said Jasmin.

"Or she's working with the shapeshifter," said Max.

That was something they didn't want to think about. Taking on a shifter and a few werewolves was one thing; but adding a very old, and very powerful witch to the equation shifted the odds sharply against them.

"First things first," said Max. "We need to figure out how to get in there."

"Leave that to us," said Jasmin. "You shift back to wolf form. Torie can keep in contact with you and Sable that way. We'll let you know when to come in."

There was a sharp rustling and cracking of sticks behind them, and as one, all three turned to face who, or what, had tried to sneak up on them.

Torie cast an orb of blue magic that illuminated Jinn in the darkness. The big elf was standing behind them, drenched in sweat and breathing hard.

"Jinn!" exclaimed Jasmin. "What are you doing out here?"

"We were attacked," he said, "by the shapeshifter and their herd of werewolves. I tried to protect Magda, but the shifter reached for me. Magda yelled for me not to let her touch me, and before I could do anything, Magda cast a spell that spirited me out of the house. I blacked out a bit and when I came to, I was far away, up on Terra Bluffs."

"Terra Bluffs? That's two counties away!" said Max. "How did you get back here?"

"I ran." The elf turned his attention to the house and started to take a step towards it.

"Jinn, wait," said Jasmin. "The house is warded by Magda's magic. Torie and I will cast a spell to bring it down."

"Save your magic. The ward recognizes me; I can get us through."

"We have friends here waiting to help," said Torie. "They will need to get in as well, once we signal them."

Reluctantly, Jinn nodded. "Fine. But be quick about it. Who knows what is happening to Magda in there?"

Torie was struck by the genuine caring in the elf's voice. Whatever his relationship to the witch, there was no doubting his loyalty to her.

She stood next to Jasmin, and the two of them lowered their heads, concentrating on their own magic. With both hands raised, they extended their own power into the ward.

"Mistress of night and mistress of day,
we ask you to let nothing stand in our way.
By your spells and enchantments and power unbound,
we ask you to bring this barrier down!"

There was a crackle of blue light that leapt from the witch's hands, colliding with the wards around the cottage. The shield bloomed, glowing richly, threatening to break under their combined power, but it held.

Together, they chanted again, pitting their might against that of the conjured barrier.

"Damn. That is some serious warding she has going on," said Jasmin.

Before they could make another attempt, a scream rang out from inside the house.

"No more time!" said Jinn. He reached out, grasping the two women in each muscular arm, and sprinted forward at a pace even a werewolf would not have been capable of matching. Before they could protest, he was past the barrier and standing on the front porch.

Standing them down, Jinn raised one leg and kicked outward, shattering the door inward.

"Yeah, next time, we'll just do that," said Jasmin, smoothing her windswept hair back into place.

They took in the scene before them in an instant. Magda was lying on her side on the floor. She was propped up on one elbow, her other hand maintaining a glowing orb of protection that shielded her from the shifter.

The shapeshifter was dressed in a hooded black robe that flowed around her as she wielded a mercurial black light with which she tried desperately to break through Magda's protective barrier.

"What are you doing here?" demanded Magda, her voice strained. "Get out of here!"

Torie wasn't sure if she was talking to them or to Jinn. Either way, she summoned a fireball and threw it at the shapeshifter, who casually lifted one hand and knocked it aside.

How was a shifter using magic, Torie wondered, even as she began looking around the room for objects to call to and use as weapons.

Jasmin lifted her hand and sent a bolt of raw power sizzling at the shifter, while Jinn picked up the large recliner by the door and tossed it at the creature. Between the two of them, they were at least able to draw her attention away from Magda.

"No, what are you doing?" cried Magda a second time. "I had her right where I wanted her!"

Just then, the shifter turned her head and let out a loud whistle.

From the back of the house, a large, silver wolf approached them. It was easily the biggest creature Torie had ever seen. Its mass took up the entire width of the hallway as it made its way into the room.

Torie closed her eyes and mentally sent a distress call.

"Max! Sable! You guys really need to get in here now!"

The wolf reared its head back and let out a piercing howl that nearly ruptured Torie's eardrums. The small cottage actually shook from the power of the call. In the distance, Torie could hear an answering howl.

He had just called for reinforcements.

Torie and Jasmin turned their attention to the shapeshifter, each calling up their magic for a simultaneous attack.

"Meat cleaver!" Torie called, holding out her hand as the large blade flew from its holder in the kitchen. Holding the knife by the handle, she whispered to it, charging it with magic until it glowed white hot.

Jasmin attacked with her magic, sending power at the shifter while Torie rushed across the space between them and slashed at the hooded figure with the knife. The blade sizzled as it struck the black light the shapeshifter used to parry the blow. But while she successfully defended the attack, she left herself open to Jasmin's powerful strikes.

Out of the corner of her eye, Torie saw the massive wolf striding towards them. She called up her magic, readying a shield that she prayed would withstand the power of such a creature.

The wolf stopped in place, his body rocked as Jinn leapt at him, slamming his fist into the beast's side. He roared in pain and turned to face the elf, jaws dripping with saliva and wild hate in his eyes.

Trying to get her bearings, Torie became aware of a

rhythmic rumble that was getting louder and louder and was beginning to shake the house. It was coming from the back side, and Torie had a feeling it was Elion.

The vampire must have been striking at the ward with all of his strength, trying to physically smash his way inside.

"Magda! Lower your wards!" screamed Torie. "Let them in to help us."

"No!" the old witch replied, making her way to her feet. "You don't understand—"

She was cut off at that point, doubling over, her hands on her head, as the wall behind her smashed inward.

Elion had indeed broken through, the wards that surrounded the house having fallen before his strength.

As soon as the barrier fell, the shifter turned her face towards the ceiling and roared in defiance. Lifting its arms, the creature rose into the air, shifting into a much larger bird of prey than any of the witches had seen before. With a single flap of wings that nearly spanned the length of the living room, she burst through the ceiling and disappeared into the night sky.

The great wolf that was with it shrugged off Jinn and bounded effortlessly through the hole in the ceiling before bounding into the woods and disappearing.

Torie and Jasmin looked at one another in shock. They weren't the only ones unsure as to what had just happened. Max and Sable were staring dumbfounded as well.

"Magda, what is going on here?" asked Jasmin. "Was that the same shapeshifter we fought earlier? And what was with that massive wolf? I've never seen one that big before."

"I have," said Max. "That was Arin. My brother."

Torie looked at him in shock. "That was your brother? The one you're planning to take out on your own?"

"To be fair, he's much bigger than I remember him being," Max replied.

"Ugh," said Magda, moaning through the pain she was obviously feeling.

Jinn rushed over to her side and gently picked her up from the floor. Moving into the part of the living room that wasn't completely destroyed, he carefully placed her on the couch, brushing a stray strand of gray hair from her face.

"You silly thing! Why did you come back? You could have been killed," she said to the elf.

He didn't reply, only smiled at her, and then made his way into the kitchen to get a glass of water for the elderly witch.

"And you two!" she said to Jasmin and Torie. "What were you thinking bursting in here like that?"

"We were thinking that we were saving you," said Torie. "It's my fault the shifter found out you had the original document."

Magda waved her hand, dismissing the conversation.

"What did you mean when you said you had the shifter where you wanted it?" asked Jasmin.

"I know what it is after now. I also know how it came to be in the state it now is." Magda leveled a look at Torie that told her the old witch did indeed know about the spell Torie had attempted.

Torie knew there was no point in denying or drawing it out any longer. "But the spell didn't work."

"Oh, it worked alright. On a very subtle front, it worked. The spell you cast not only ate away at the fated-mate bond, but it also ate away at the bond that all shifters, especially wolves, share. Alpha and beta for instance. And more importantly, the link that a pack shares with its alpha."

"I felt that," said Max, emphatically. "I wasn't sure what exactly I was feeling, but something was…broken."

"What are you talking about?" said Sable. "What spell?"

Reluctantly, Torie told them all what she had done. To her dismay, no one chastised her for her actions; and more importantly for her, no one looked at her with pity.

Sable offered her the slightest of smiles. "I love that you think you needed magic to hold onto him. And I hate that I put you in that situation in the first place."

She moved to stand next to Torie and gave her a hug. "Thank you. For trying at least. That means more to us—" she glanced at Elion, "—than you can know." She then turned her attention back to Magda. "But that still doesn't explain how Arin got to be so big."

The old witch fixed her steely gray eyes on Max. "That wolf is not your brother. Not anymore at least. Your brother as you knew him is dead."

A chill settled over the room as Magda's words undoubtedly created more questions than answers.

"I gave the shifter the spell," she told them. When no one questioned her, she continued. "I needed to know what it wanted with it. Then, once I knew the creature's endgame, I could have stopped it."

"Let me guess; we messed that up," said Jasmin.

Magda didn't respond. Instead, she released a heavy sigh and shook her head.

"I was a fool. I should not have done that. I'm old; not the witch I once was," she replied.

"What happened here?" asked Torie.

"The shifter did indeed attack. I sent Jinn away because I didn't want him getting hurt, or killed, in the confrontation. The shifter said it knew I had the original spell and wanted it. It wanted to cast a binding spell that was capable of trapping shifters in their original forms. It already possessed the pages from the grimoire that contained the reversal spells, and it intended to destroy them…so the spell would be permanent.

"It said that was the only way to finally be at peace."

Magda shook her head sadly and looked from Jasmin to Torie. "I was right about it being a chimera. But I didn't realize just how deep this creature's affliction ran. A magical chimera is literally two beings in one. The chimera was in turmoil as both parts of their self were fighting for dominance. The shifter wanted to split itself back into two beings, once and for all."

Jasmin swallowed hard, trying to follow what the witch was saying. "You mean, literally, one shifter, becomes two?"

Magda nodded. "In this case, one part of the chimera was a shifter, the other half was a witch."

"That would explain why a shifter was able to wield magic as well," said Torie.

"Yes," continued Magda, "that part could cast the spells that would free each of them. The peaceful coexistence they were experiencing is beginning to fray. Being free of one another was not something they had ever considered a possibility. Now, it is all they can think about."

"But how long has this been going on?" asked Torie.

"Well, they were born the way they are. So, from birth. But my guess is that while one may have always been aware of the other, it wasn't until recently that they fell into conflict."

She didn't say anything else. She didn't have to.

Torie nodded slowly. "Not until I cast that spell. I set this all into motion." She clasped a hand to her mouth. "Oh no. I'm the reason Alma was killed. I'm the reason all of this conflict started!"

Jasmin took her by the hand and squeezed hard. "Stop it! No, you aren't the cause of this."

Magda shrugged both shoulders and grimaced. "Well, if you want to get technical about it—"

"Read the room, Magda," said Sable, butting in. "If this is her fault, then it's mine as well. I was hiding out in Trinity, which is where Arin tracked me to. That's got to be where he met this shifter."

"Yes, a creature like that would have relished the anonymity that Trinity Falls would provide. There are limitless shadows in a town like that in which it could hide," agreed Magda.

"But now it's here. And you let it cast that spell?" asked Jasmin.

"The spell allowed it to revert back to its original form. In the case of this chimera, that is the form it had in the womb. Two distinct beings. However, there was no other body for half of it to inhabit," said Magda.

"Of course," said Jasmin. "It needed a host."

Magda was nodding. "That was where Arin came in to play. The shifter had brought the wolf with it when it attacked. What Arin thought he was getting out of the deal I have no idea. But I'm sure it wasn't the ending he expected.

"The half of the chimera that was shifter went into Arin's body and made it its own. The other half, the witch half, imbued the shifter with great power, hence the physical change. The witch side of the shifter was what I was fighting when you came in. I'm pretty sure that's the one calling all the shots."

"What were you trying to do?" asked Jasmin.

"After the spell that separated them, I wanted to put

them back together; permanently. Once I understood what they wanted to accomplish, I thought I could undo it."

"You were going to reverse the spell. Even though the shifter undoubtedly destroyed the spell that could do that," said Jasmin.

Magda nodded again. "My vanity coupled with my desire for revenge. That monster killed my sister in cold blood."

"Then we find them and finish what you started," said Torie.

"It won't be that easy," said Magda. "There was one thing about the spell that you misinterpreted. There is a way to make the separation permanent; so that no reversal can change it. That was what the shapeshifter was after."

Torie frowned as terrifying thoughts rushed through her head. "The ward you had up...that wasn't to keep anything from getting into your house, was it? It was to keep them from getting out."

Magda stared at her, eyes twinkling in agreement.

"Magda, what does the shifter have to do to make the spell permanent?" asked Torie.

"At this point, all they would need to do is kill an innocent as an act of blatant violence."

"So, that explains what they wanted with Fionna." said Jasmin.

"Oh no," said Torie, her face a mask of horror. "They're going to use her as their sacrificial lamb."

Chapter Twenty-Four

"Come on, Torie. Concentrate. You can do this."

They were words of encouragement uttered from Jasmin as she tried to provide as much support as possible.

Torie was floating in mid-air, her legs tucked beneath her as she focused her magic on finding Elric. Her hex power allowed her to communicate with shifters in their animal form, but she had not been able to reach Fionna. Which meant that she was either in her human form, or she was dead.

But her connection with Elric ran deeper. Their rapport allowed her an awareness of him, and vice versa, that was not dependent on him being in wolf form.

Still, she had never tried to purposefully reach him via that bond, and especially not over so great a distance. But it was the only hope they had for finding Fionna, assuming that he was with her. Max could no longer sense his beta's whereabouts either; with the link they shared severed, he had no way of tracking his ex-lieutenant.

While Torie attempted to find him through their

connection, Elion stood outside the house, still as a statue, breathing in the night air. Dawn was quickly approaching, and while it would not kill him, the sun would greatly diminish his senses. He sifted through the countless smells that he could detect, trying desperately to lock onto Elric or Fionna.

Everyone was doing their part as the clock ticked down for their friend.

Eldritch energy glowed and swirled around Torie as she probed further and further with her mind, reaching for her lover.

And then she felt it. A warmth. A familiarity. A calmness in a sea of turbulence that was unmistakable.

"Elric," she whispered. She could feel him, but everything around him was dark. Was he conscious? His normally hyper-acute senses felt dull to her. Unsure what to do, she probed deeper into his mind, prodding him to open his eyes and look around.

She could feel the spark of consciousness and stoked it into a roaring furnace, bringing it to life.

"I've got him," she said.

"Where is he?" asked Jasmin.

Torie probed further, looking at what he had seen previously as well as readying herself for what might come through in real time. She felt him open his eyes, and a rush of images flooded Torie's mind. Jasmin had already cast a spell that would project what Torie saw into the air and immediately the entrance to what looked like a dark, overgrown cave, with wooden beams supporting the entrance filled the air.

"That's definitely the old mining encampment. It's very unstable. Hopefully, Elric is there as well. He could have already found Fionna." said Jasmin.

In a flash, Elion was gone, running faster than the eye could follow.

"What about us!" said Torie to Jasmin. "We can't magically transport everyone there."

"Maybe not, but I can." It was Magda speaking. The old witch raised both arms into the air, which crackled and bloomed with magic around her. "Portal magic is a forgotten art it seems."

The old witch hummed, changing the pitch of her voice with the changes in the color of the magic that thrummed around her until it was a pale gold and orange, like that of the most perfect of sunsets.

Then, she reached out with both hands and grabbed the glowing light, pulling it wide and stretching it just as an artist might when they shaped red-hot glass into fine pieces of art. She created a large ring with her magic and tossed it through the room, enlarging it as it moved until it formed a large gate in the middle of the living area.

Everyone watched as it shimmered in the air, the opening growing translucent until they could see the opening to the mines that Torie had pulled from Elric's mind.

"You have got to teach me that," said Jasmin, as she admired the older witch's handiwork.

Sweat beaded along Magda's brow, and she was breathing hard as her arms began to tremor.

"Hurry. Everybody through. Not sure how long I can keep this open."

Torie had a brief moment where she considered the danger they could all be stepping into. This was all her fault, and she should be the one to fix it. But it was that kind of thinking that led her to make bad decisions.

She was done with that train of thinking. Like or not,

she had a new family now. The likes of which she had never imagined before.

And right now, one of them was in mortal danger.

The best bet Torie had of saving Fionna meant embracing her made family; so she gritted her teeth, grasped hands with Jasmin, and stepped through the portal.

It felt like walking through water for the briefest of moments, and then they were facing the opening to the mine, the cool night air blowing gently across their skin. It was a beautiful and quiet night; one that would have been perfect for a nice cocktail if it weren't for the fact there was death and destruction crowding the backs of their minds.

There was a soft pop in the air, and the two of them turned to see Magda, Jinn, Max and Sable stepping through as well.

"You don't have to do this," said Torie. "I can't bear the thought of anyone else getting hurt because of something I did. We will handle this."

"Of that I have little doubt," said Magda.

"But you won't be doing it alone," added Max.

There was no time for debating the situation as they were all greeted by low, rumbling growls that came from all around them, echoing from the dark woods.

"Looks like my brother's pack is providing security," said Max. He held up a hand and slowly extended razor-sharp claws as he morphed into his hybrid werewolf form.

Sable stood beside him, shifting to full wolf, and letting go with her own menacing growl.

"You guys go make with the magic," said Max, his voice half snarl at this point. "We will keep these wolves busy." He looked at Sable and nodded. As one, they leapt for the woods, letting loose a roar and a howl that caused the hair on the back of Torie's arms to stand up.

"Go. Help them," Magda said to Jinn. The elf looked at her reluctantly, then gave a hard glance to Torie and Jasmin, as if to say 'protect her, or else'. Then he simply nodded and charged into the darkened undergrowth after Max and Sable.

Once alone, the three witches headed towards the mouth of the mine and stepped through, walking towards the dim light that shone in the distance. They moved as silently as they could, focusing on the sound of voices that were barely audible from ahead.

"...another way is all I'm saying. I'm not sure this is the right thing to do," said a deep, male voice.

"That isn't you talking!" said a female voice. The witches recognized it as that of the shapeshifter they had fought previously.

"It's all so confusing," said the male.

"No, it isn't. That wolf, the shifter you are locked within, is the one having those thoughts. Not you. Don't you remember what it was like before? The noise? The chaos we experienced when we were in one body. Do you want to go back to that?"

The male didn't say anything, but the witches could hear shuffling around, before the shifter mumbled a few more words that they could not understand.

"It just seems wrong to do this to her. She looks helpless there. And...this male seems familiar to me as well. He came to help her..."

There was the sharp sound of flesh smacking flesh, followed by a soft whimper.

"Snap out of it. Everything we've done up to this point has been to benefit both of us! Look at us! We are in two separate bodies; we are having a conversation that isn't taking place inside one mind. We can't—we *won't*—go back to that."

There was a threat implied in the words that was crystal clear, and it gave Torie an idea. She looked at Jasmin and could tell that she was thinking the same thing as well. Magda looked at the two of them like they were crazy, wrinkling her brow in question.

There was no time to explain to her, and no way of doing so without alerting the shifter to their presence. Not that it would have mattered; a long, soulless howl reverberated through the mine, bouncing off every piece of rock in the place.

"What was that? What is going on?" the shifter asked.

"It's my pack—or rather his pack," said the wolf shifter. "They've been attacked! I need to go help them!"

"Don't be an idiot. If they have been attacked, then that means the witches are probably here. Though I have no idea how. Either way, we need to finish this now. We have two victims, so we each kill one. Then nothing can ever undo what we have become."

That was all the three witches needed to hear. They entered the chamber just beyond where they crouched, taking in the scene before them.

Elric was in a heap against one wall. A large gash across his forehead leaked blood into his eyes. He was clearly disoriented, his head lolling back and forth as he tried to focus on the witches. In front of him was a large wooden table, on top of which lay Fionna. She was shackled by her ankles and wrists to crude-looking restraints that had reverse barbs digging cruelly into the shifter's flesh.

"I wondered where you were," said the female, her head snapping up to face the witches. She turned toward the male, who the witches now knew was none other than Arin; Max's brother. "We should have killed them sooner."

Her eyes began to glow yellow, and her lips moved in silent recitation of an incantation that summoned a rotating ring of light before her. With a heave she sent it spinning towards the table Fionna was bound to. Torie screamed and dove in front of the hissing disc. She did not have a chance to throw up a shield and instinctively threw her body over Fionna's, hugging her friend's head to her as she waited for the impact of something she was pretty sure would cleave her in two.

The hit never came.

Instead, Magda appeared in front of Torie. She used the tip of her cane to block the light; hooking the ring and throwing it high into the air where it crashed into the ceiling gouging out a considerable hunk of rock.

"Careful now," she said, her eyes locking with those of the woman, "you don't want to bring this crashing down on your head, do you?" With that, she waved her cane in the air, summoning a swirl of blue power that she aimed at the woman and Arin.

Torie could feel the blast of power arching out of Magda. She hoped it would give her time to free Fionna. She concentrated on the restraints and closed her eyes.

"Binds of steel, iron or ore,
heed my plea, and be no more."

The chains that held Fionna turned to mist, melting off her bleeding flesh as they dissolved to the floor. Torie shook Fionna, trying to rouse her in order to get the squirrel shifter to her feet.

A flash of light lit up the inside of the mine as Magda

was struck with a bolt of power that threw her savagely against the far wall where she crumpled, unmoving.

"You know, I wanted to kill the squirrel because she was born and raised in this community. I don't know if killing a witch will have the same effect on the spell, but I'm willing to find out," said the woman, turning her attention to Magda's crumpled body.

Before she could do anything, she was surrounded by crimson rings that enclosed her, wrapping around her legs, waist and upper body, pinning her arms at her side. Behind her, Jasmin had her eyes closed as she brought her hands together, mimicking the ethereal chains that she summoned to hold the woman tight.

"No!" the shapeshifter screamed, struggling against the power Jasmin had summoned. "Help me, brother," she cried to Arin. "They will ruin everything we have worked so hard for!"

There was a rumble in the air as the man shifted into his enormous wolf form. He approached Jasmin slowly, the deep warning rumble in his chest reverberating off the rock walls.

Jasmin struggled to maintain the binding spell she had cast. There was no way she could hold the shapeshifter in place and fend off the wolf.

She was about to release the shifter when Torie stepped up behind the wolf.

"Arin! Stop this. You don't have to do this; I heard what you said. You are right...it is wrong what you are being asked to do." She held up both hands, drawing the wolf's attention from Jasmin.

Arin stopped, his breath hot and foul as it billowed from his nostrils. Torie listened for his thoughts, trying to establish a connection.

"Arin, I know you're in there. I can feel you; your influence is still there. I know you came here to settle unfinished business with your brother; and somehow it turned into this madness. That shapeshifter used you as a means to her ends —she had no interest in helping you accomplish yours."

The great wolf shook its head from side to side, howling in reply. Then, slowly, almost painfully, it shifted back into human form.

"I can't..." Arin said, swaying on his feet as he held his hands to his head. "They are so strong, and more than anything they don't want to be put back into one body. He's...he's fighting me at every turn. Each minute I'm losing more and more of me. I can't feel my pack. I can't feel anything...he's controlling them now..."

"Arin, let us help you fight them." Torie looked over her shoulder to see that Jasmin was struggling with being able to contain the shapeshifter.

"I can't hold her much longer," said Jasmin, her voice strained.

Torie turned her attention back to Arin. "There is a way to recombine them. Magda knows how to reverse the spell. She tried it at her house but wasn't able to finish it. Can you help us?"

"She's lying!" screamed the shapeshifter. "That spell will not reverse what I did. It will undo us completely! They seek to kill us, brother."

Arin threw back his head and roared in pain. His body began to contort as the wolf inside him struggled to be free. Torie knew if he succeeded in shifting, they may never get Arin back again.

She reached out with her mind, casting a hex into the wolf to stun him. It shot out like a dagger from her and pierced deep into his mind, stunning him. She could sense the two natures inside him, and she wondered if this was the pain the shapeshifter had lived through. No wonder she had been so desperate to pull them apart. Just grazing Arin's tortured mind was almost too much for her to handle.

"Magda!" she screamed in the direction of the old witch. "Get up! We can't do this without you...reverse the spell!"

The old witch was moving slowly, trying to gather her wits about her. But Torie knew she was in no shape to cast the kind of spell needed to stop this madness. She looked at Jasmin and saw how she struggled; the shapeshifter's eyes were glowing, and she was calling on her own magic to break free.

It was only a matter of time.

Torie swallowed hard, closed her eyes, and did the only thing she could think of.

"Through a sea of tears, let hearts be broken,
I take back the words that I have spoken.
Let the law of nature hear this deal,
and to those that should be, I un- bind their wills.
By the light of the moon, and that of the sun,
let no creature be bound by the desires of one.
Goddess of nature from which we hail,
I implore you now, let free will prevail."

She held out her hands, and then brought them together forcefully. A mystical shockwave blasted forth, striking everyone within the space and then echoing outward, rippling through the mountain and surrounding terrain.

She felt the effects almost immediately. The fighting that was going on outside among the wolves stopped immediately, and she could sense them converging at the mouth of the opening, searching for their alpha.

For his part, Arin remained human, but then, his body went rigid and crashed face first to the floor. At the same time, the shapeshifter stopped struggling in Jasmin's grasp, her body going limp as well. Slowly, Jasmin released her, letting the magical bindings gently lower her body to the ground.

"Torie, what did you just do?" Jasmin asked.

"Maybe we can't break the fated-mate bond. But we can give those touched by it the right to choose. They can choose to accept the bond or reject it with no consequences. From now on, no supernatural decides their own fate. And that includes the alpha's as well," siad Torie. Her voice was melodious, still filled with the power of her spell.

"She created a new binding is what she did," said Magda. The old witch held her side and inched slowly closer to them. "You didn't reverse it; and your hex has forced the minds of the chimera back together. I've never felt anything like that. What are you?"

Torie shook her head like she was clearing away cobwebs as she turned to look at her friends.

"What? What are you talking about? You know what I am."

"I know what I thought you were, child. But what you just did? That will be felt for some time to come. You've just created a new Law of Nature, and I have no idea how it will play out."

Just then, their friends entered the space, looking around at the scene unfolding before them.

"What happened here?" asked Max, looking at his brother's form. "Is he..."

"No, he's alive," said Magda. "But he may well wish he weren't."

A moan floated to their ears, and they turned to see the shapeshifter slowly gaining consciousness. Her eyes grew wide in despair and her face twisted into a mask of rage.

"What have you done? Where is my brother? I swear, before all that is unholy, I am going to kill you all."

Magda held out her hand, calling her cane to her. Then, moving it slowly in a circle around the shapeshifter's head, she whispered an incantation that froze the creature where she sat.

"What now?" asked Jasmin. "How long will that work?"

"Long enough for me to do what must be done," said Magda with a sigh. She turned to Torie. "The spell you cast has destroyed the half of the chimera that was shifter. That was the less dominant half, so to speak, so in resetting the Law of Nature as you did, it was no longer able to exist. The unfortunate thing is, I fear that Arin's mind was wiped out with it as well. He was singularly fixated on disrupting another aspect of the original Law of Nature—namely, the fated mate bond.

"What you did, not only changed that bond, but also that which made him an alpha. Like I said, I have no idea what you have done, what long-ranging effects it will have. But all I know is that the chimera has been driven mad by the loss of her other self. There will come a time when she finds a way to be free of the body she currently inhabits. And she will come after you and your loved ones."

"Yes," said Torie. "I don't know how, but I can feel it. She is already resisting Magda's magics."

"Okay, how are you feeling all of this?" asked Jasmin. "And how do you know about any of this, Magda?"

"Shh," said the old witch. "You need to go. All of you,

get out of here. There is only one thing left to do, and I have to do it now before she frees herself!"

Before anyone could answer, she brought the heel of her cane down onto the rock floor, striking it hard enough that the shaft of the mine vibrated. There was a rumble in the distance as the old woman's eyes glowed with power. She looked at them and smiled, just as lightning struck the mountainside above them, causing the entire shaft to shiver as tons of rock and debris began to collapse inward.

Chapter Twenty-Five

"Everyone out of here!" screamed Jasmin.

She ran to the table where Fionna still lay and scooped her up, dropping one arm around her shoulder. dragging the unconscious shifter along with her. Torie did the same with Elric. The wolf was coming around and was thankfully able to shuffle along with her, but the witches knew they would never make it out of the mine in time.

Sable's shifter strength allowed her to throw Arin over her shoulders and run for the entrance of the cave with Max and Jinn close behind her. She ran out, just as the heavy timbers that framed the mouth of the mine began to crack under the weight of the shifting mine.

It was coming down on top of them.

Max dived for the opening and shifted to his hybrid form. He braced the beams over his head, his muscles straining with the effort of holding them up. Jinn joined him, using all his formidable elfin strength to also hold open the entrance.

They groaned with the effort as Torie and Jasmin made

their way towards them. Through gritted teeth and squinted eyes, they saw the mine filling with more falling rock and choking dust as it started collapsing. The wolf and the elf felt their strength giving out and knew they could not keep the mine open long enough for the witches and their friends to get through.

Then, just as they were about to break, they felt the weight above them lessen. Opening their eyes, they saw Elion standing there, taking on the weight the two of them had been shouldering.

"Go!" he said. "Help them get out. I'll hold this!"

Without a second thought, the wolf and the elf raced forward to grab Fionna and Elric, freeing up Torie and Jasmin to run for the opening. Together, they all dove through the mouth of the mineshaft, just as everything collapsed behind them. It sounded like a freight train had roared through the underground compartment as everything went black.

Looking back, they saw Elion stepping away just as the entrance was covered by the sinking mountainside, sealing the entrance away behind tons of rock and debris.

Jinn ran towards the opening, screaming. He fell to his knees and began clawing at the earth, heaving aside rocks and wood in an effort to reopen the entrance.

Jasmin, breathing hard, moved to stand behind the big elf and reached out slowly, placing her hand on his shoulder. Eventually, he stopped clawing at the earth and looked up at her, his face wet with tears. Jasmin shook her head slowly at him, letting him know it was no use.

All she could do was hug his head to her bosom and let him cry as his body was racked with spasms and pain.

Torie walked over to them. Before she could say anything, a warm wind blew through them, and Torie gasped, her eyes radiating a warm blue light. She stepped back and turned her face to the sky.

"Do not mourn me, my friend," she said, her words directed at Jinn. *"While our time together in this plane has come to an end, it does not mean I won't see you again one day. Until then, take care of my garden. Our garden. And know that I have treasured your friendship more than you will ever know. Thank you, my Jinn; my friend."*

Then, the wind subsided, and she was gone. Torie stepped back, weakened and awed by what had just happened.

"So, what now?" asked Jasmin.

"Well, the first thing we need to do is get the shifters in town back together for a follow up meeting," said Torie. "We need to let them know about the changes that some of them may or may not be impacted by. Moving forward, Singing Falls will be a sanctuary town...but nothing will be forced. It will be a sanctuary because everyone will be safe and protected under the eyes of the law. If punishment is deemed necessary, it will fit the crime."

They were all back at Torie's house, sitting in the great room, sipping on strong coffee. The sun was just beginning to peak over the hillside, turning the sky to a beautiful golden yellow. Torie had agreed to let Elion stay in one of her guest rooms for the day. It was the least she could do after he had saved them from a crushing death.

She sat on the loveseat, Leo curled up on her lap and Elric resting beside her.

"I agree. But we need to let them know that this time, there won't be any interruptions by crazed shape shifters looking to maim and kill," said Jasmin. "Why don't we have this one at my house. Change of place could equal change of mindset for some who may be reluctant to return."

Torie nodded. "Agreed. Besides, I need to replace some windows in here. Again."

Jasmin laughed. "The local contractors are starting to love you."

"Well, I don't know about you all, but I'm heading home to my wife and about three days in a hot bath," said Fionna, getting up and stretching her arms overhead.

"Please have that wound on your head checked," said Torie. "You and Glen have been through the ringer lately. You both need to rest."

"And we will. For a bit. But then, we start the renovations on the bakery! Promise me that; because I have so many ideas, and I want to have it ready for the wine festival in a couple of months."

There was no way either Torie or Jasmin could say no to the look of joy in her eyes. They both just laughed and nodded, which seemed to make Fionna's morning as she clapped her hands gleefully and headed out the door.

"We should offer her a ride," said Jasmin.

"I'm fine," called Fionna through the closed door.

"Well, at least we know her hearing is back to normal," said Torie.

They were silent for a moment as they sipped their coffee and contemplated the night's events.

"And what about us?" said Jasmin. "Are we back to normal?"

Torie swallowed another sip of her drink and smiled at her friend. "Always."

"I don't know," said Elric. "You two are usually in lock-step, but I kinda got the feeling you were on separate sides of the fence on this one. It's good to see that you moved past that."

"Oh yeah? And what about you, Mister? You were all about running out and playing wolf assassin with Max," said Jasmin.

"Well, that's because someone messed with my head," he said playfully, nuzzling at Torie.

She didn't smile and felt her cheeks grow hot. "I will never do that again. You will never know how much I regret doing that."

Immediately, Elric changed his tone, taking her hand in his. "Torie, I am sorry. I didn't mean to make you feel bad. We are all new to this world. I mean, all I've ever known are wolves. I don't know anything about witches. And all you've ever known are humans. We're bound to step in it from time to time when trying to navigate these waters. All we can do is remember what we mean to each other and always promise to give one another grace when we need to."

Torie felt a tear slip down her cheek as she leaned forward, touching her forehead against his.

"Wow, you guys are nauseating," said Jasmin with a warm chuckle. "But you're also really good for each other. And it makes me realize that I have to give grace as well. I've been in the world of supernaturals a lot longer than you, Torie. Not that it makes me an expert at all...if anything, it makes me realize I need to listen to others and their opinions even more."

The door opened just then, and Max and Sable entered the great room. Torie looked at them with concern as they plopped down on two of the chairs in the room.

"How is he?" she asked.

"No change," said Max. "Whatever happened to him in there is deeper than we thought. His pack can't sense him anymore. They are saying it feels like he's dead; even though his body is alive."

"Next steps?" asked Jasmin.

"Well, we were talking about that. We are taking him back up north, to the territories in Maine. I don't think it will change anything with him, but his pack needs to know he is there," said Max.

"And as for leadership...maybe it's time someone else tried to unite the two packs up there into one. Something like that has always been feared, but now...times are changing. I think the right leader could make it happen."

"And who will be that leader?" asked Torie.

Max smiled and gestured towards Sable. "You're looking at her. She's alpha material if I've ever seen it."

Elric cleared his throat. "I agree. I can feel it as well. I think that is part of why we felt the need to resist our bond so greatly. She was destined to lead, and to take another alpha as her mate. Not me."

"But your mate is...not a wolf," said Jasmin. "How will that work?"

She shrugged in response. "Times have changed. Elion will be joining us in a few days, and we will see how the pack responds to having a vampire in their midst. But I intend to make this work. With a little help from my friends."

"Your friends?" said Torie. "I'm flattered...but Jasmin and I have—"

"No, no. Not you two. The pack might be ready to accept a vampire in their midst, but we aren't going to push the envelope with witches. Not just yet," she said.

"She means us," said Elric, standing up and nodding at Max. "Both packs are familiar with us. If she shows up with just the comatose body of an ex-alpha...well, that could raise some hard suspicions. But together, they may listen to us."

He stopped talking and looked at Torie.

"How long will you be gone for?" she asked.

"Not sure. But hopefully not more than a couple of weeks. It's been a while. Max and I have people we really need to reconnect with." He placed a hand on her head and trailed it down to her cheek. "But only as long as you are okay with it."

She held his hand and smiled. "Go for as long as you need. And if you need anything from me, just call."

"And what will you two be up to while we are out?" asked Max.

Jasmin let out a long sigh. "Rest. Lots of rest. Before re-opening a new bakery in town, that is."

"And I would like to swing by to check in on Jinn. He suffered a traumatic loss; the least we can do is have him over for dinner."

Elric frowned. "If you do that, can you at least make sure he puts some clothes on?"

Everyone laughed at that, but then Elric's eyes softened and fell on Torie. "See, your heart is always in the right place. That's why I love you so much."

Torie blushed again, flustered by his remarks. Before she could say anything, he planted a kiss on her mouth and winked at her, then headed out the door with Sable and Max behind him.

"Wait!" yelled Torie, jumping up to rush to the door. "Elric, there is one thing I need to ask you. And I don't know if it's fair to bring it up now, but I need to know…"

The werewolf stopped and waited for Max and Sable to pass by before he stepped close to her in the doorway.

"Anything, Torie. What is it?"

She took a deep breath and looked him in the eyes. "It's…well, it's stupid but…Alma left Fionna—I know, long story—because she was going to get old at a normal human rate and Fionna wasn't. She felt guilty about staying with a shifter that doesn't age the same. So, I look at us and wonder…well, I wonder if that will bother you someday?"

Elric cocked his head to one side and then pulled her into his embrace, breathing in her scent deeply.

"I don't care about age, Torie. Be it ten years from now, or a hundred; you will always be beautiful to me."

Torie exhaled sharply and felt her body relax. She gave him a squeeze and a quick kiss.

"I love you, Elric."

"And I you."

He left to join Max and Sable in Max's truck, throwing one last look at Torie.

Once they were gone, Torie and Jasmin picked up the coffee cups and headed into the kitchen with them. Torie loaded them into the dishwasher before turning to her friend.

"I'm torn, Jasmin. Do we tell Jinn?"

"Tell him what? That Magda is probably not dead? That she collapsed the mountain around them to create a prison that the chimera will never be able to escape from? And that she has to remain there, pretty much as her jailor for all time? No. No good will come of that. We couldn't help Magda now no matter how much we want to. He certainly can't do anything for her; but he will never stop trying. Better to let him grieve and recover in time."

Torie nodded as she started the washer. When Magda had reached out to her and she relayed her goodbye to Jinn, she was connected to the old witch in a way that let her experience everything Magda was experiencing. When she told Jasmin what was happening, they had both agreed there was nothing either of them could do.

At least not at the moment.

"Hey, I have an idea," said Jasmin. "Fionna is down and out for a few days. your man is out of the picture as well. In a couple of weeks, we are going to be elbow-deep in inspectors and contractors and pastry flour. Why don't you and I pack up your little monster—er, dragon—and take off for a few days? Just a girls' road trip. I know a beautiful bed and breakfast out at the shore where we can relax and unwind for a few days."

Torie considered her friend's words and slowly began to nod her head. They could use some time away from everything.

And she had a feeling it would do them both some good to be away from Singing Falls for a bit. Just the two of them.

She smiled. After all, what's the worst that could happen?

Next in the Singing Falls Witches Series

vinci-books.com/singlewitch

A road trip, a luxury spa, and no magic—what could go wrong?

For witches Torie and Jasmin, plenty. When death and danger lurk, they'll need more than a getaway to solve this supernatural mystery.

Turn the page for a free preview…

Hex and the Single Witch:
Chapter One

"Are you sure you're okay with this?" Torie questioned. "I mean, it's only a long weekend, but still."

Elric laughed softly and turned over to face her, using one hand to softly push a strand of hair out of her eyes.

"I think I'll be fine," he said. "Besides, you don't need my permission to go on a girls' trip with Jasmin."

Torie frowned. "Is that what it sounded like? That I was asking permission? I wasn't. I just didn't want to say I was doing it as if you had no opinion on the matter."

"Oh? And what if I said no, I didn't want you to go?"

Torie laughed. "Well, you'd get over it."

Elric smiled and rolled over, stretching. "It's fine. Besides, I may have to make a quick trip back up north to help with a council matter. So, I probably won't even be here when you get back."

Torie got up, quickly reaching for her robe and throwing it around her before standing.

"Why do you do that?" Elric asked.

Torie felt heat rise into her cheeks, and she was glad he couldn't see her face.

"How's that going? Establishing a new council to lead a new pack of werewolves made up of two previously warring clans can't be easy," she said. It was clear she was trying to change the subject and she knew it wouldn't work.

"Don't deflect," Elric said. "I find you so beautiful and yet you always seem in a hurry to get dressed."

Torie sighed and turned to face her boyfriend. He had moved to the top of the covers and was sprawled out naked on the bed.

"See, I don't think I will ever be that comfortable in my skin. It must be a wolf thing."

Elric nodded. "You're right. Shifters are more comfortable naked than in clothes. We feel less confined. I just wish you could see yourself the way I do."

Torie sighed and wished that were possible. She knew she still carried baggage with her from her failed marriage. She was aware that it might be baggage she would carry forever, but she was trying.

Her ex-husband had never wanted to see her naked and made it a point of telling her to cover up. He also had been the type to always remind her to not eat so much bread when they were out, and to ask when her next Pilates or aerobics class was. Thinking back on this now, she realized he probably wanted to know where she was at all times so he could plan his sneaking around with another woman behind her back.

Well, that had certainly come back to bite him. He was spending the next twenty-five years to life in a federal prison because of that decision. She knew she should have felt bad for him, but she just couldn't.

She had finally found the strength to forgive him for his

affair, and that was about as good as she could be in the situation. She had spent so long thinking horrible thoughts about him and wishing ill on the man, that she now felt ashamed of herself for putting such things out into the universe. The fact that she had nearly died saving his child and his fae mistress more than balanced the karmic scales as far as she was concerned.

During her trip down memory lane, Elric had moved to the edge of the bed to sit next to her. He placed an arm around her waist, pulling her into him.

For a second, Torie flinched, reflexively reaching for his hand to move it from her side. She could hear her ex's words clearly in her mind the morning he mentioned something about a muffin top and then laughed it off.

But this wasn't him. This was a real man; one who had accepted her and her muffin top and made her feel like she was the most important person in his world.

She leaned over and kissed him.

"Thank you," she said.

"For?"

"Being you. You never cease to amaze me."

He smiled and stretched languidly. "Thank you. But don't change the subject. I know what you need. I have a great idea." His eyes twinkled mischievously.

"And what might that be?" she asked, a slight frown making its way across her features.

"We are having a naked weekend as soon as we are both back from our trips."

Torie had to fight the urge to let her mouth drop open. "I'm sorry. A what?"

"You know. A naked weekend. We are going to spend the entire weekend naked. I'll stock up the fridge and make sure we have everything we need so we don't even have to leave the house."

Torie fought to suppress the laughing fit she felt coming on. The look on her boyfriend's face told her he was absolutely serious, however.

She patted him on the chest as she made her way towards the bathroom. "You hold onto that thought. I'm going to shower and get dressed. Jasmin should be here soon to pick me up. We need to get going; we still need to drop Leo off at Fionna's."

"I feel bad I can't stay here with the little guy," Elric said.

"Don't even worry about it. He gets along great with Fionna, and she is ecstatic about keeping him for a few days."

Finding a dragon sitter wasn't easy, and Torie was thankful that Fionna got along so well with her pet.

She made her way into the bath, careful to shut the door behind her before dropping her towel.

"Hold up. He said what?" Jasmin asked.

She and Torie were in the kitchen, packing some snacks and bottles of water, and a few last-minute road trip items they may need.

Torie looked around making sure Elric wasn't within earshot. Of course, with werewolf hearing, she was pretty sure he could hear them from outside if he wanted to.

"He said he wants to have a naked weekend when I get back," Torie said.

Jasmin roared with laughter. "Girl, that is some wolf nonsense right there. I told you what could happen if you started dating one, but oh no, you had to get your swerve on with a supernatural."

Torie playfully flung a paperback at her friend.

"Keep your voice down! And why aren't you appalled at the idea?"

"What is there to be appalled at? He's not wrong; you are a bit of a prude."

Torie was about to answer when she heard the front door chime. Elric entered the kitchen, smiling at Jasmin.

"Okay, all Torie's stuff is loaded in the back. You two are all set. Although, I have to ask, what's with all the pillows? They don't have those where you're staying?"

"Of course they do," said Jasmin. "But I need *my* pillow. I can't sleep on a different one."

"Same here," said Torie. "It's an age thing."

"Well, I hope you guys have a great time. Don't think about this place at all. For the next few days, Singing Falls and all its craziness is not your concern," he said.

Torie couldn't help but frown a bit. "Well, I mean, everyone does have our number in the event that something happens, right?"

Elric rolled his eyes playfully. "Of course they do. But nothing will happen. And even if it does, Max is more than capable of dealing with things on his own."

Torie let out a deep breath. He was right. The town's resident werewolf sheriff had more than proven himself lately. Still, she had grown to love everyone in this community and couldn't help but worry. Something rubbed against her shin, and she looked down to see Leo pressing his weight against her, his wings shimmering as he pined for her attention.

She patted her shoulder and the little dragon lifted off

the ground and landed on her arm, making his way up to perch on her shoulder, nuzzling into her hair.

"And I'll only be up north with Sable for a bit. Then I'll be back to help keep an eye on things as well," said Elric, reaching forward to scratch under Leo's chin.

"And you'll call if you need something?" Torie questioned.

Before he could answer, Jasmin took her by the hand to drag her out of the kitchen.

"No, he won't call," she said, turning to glance back at Elric. "If anything comes up that you can't handle, well... too bad. Deal with it until we get back. But do not call her."

They were out of the house and piling into Jasmin's sleek new Jaguar drop top when Elric caught up with them. He handed a paper bag to Torie with a smile.

"I picked this up this morning for you. They are the last of the elderberry scones from Jim's. He wanted you to have them."

Torie couldn't help but smile as she opened the bag and inhaled the aroma of the freshly baked scones.

"Oh my. Thank you! That was so thoughtful, Elric."

He shrugged in response. "It was nothing. I knew that with this being the last weekend the bakery will be open, you'd miss them. Although I hear Fionna has almost badgered Jim into giving her the recipe for them."

Torie laughed in response. If anyone could convince the former owner of the bakery to give one of his most prized recipes to the new owner, it would be Fionna.

Torie sighed as she wrapped her arms around Elric. He was right. She needed a break and some down time. Taking over the bakery with Fionna and Jasmin would eat up much of her free time when she returned.

This might be her last chance to get away for some time.

Elric gave her a squeeze and planted a kiss on the top of her forehead. She breathed in his scent and looked up into his eyes.

"I'll see you in a few days," Torie whispered to him.

He nodded before releasing her and opening the car door for her. Bending down, he smiled in Jasmin's direction as she climbed behind the wheel. "Have fun, safe trip."

"Don't worry. I'll take good care of her. I won't let her do anything I wouldn't do myself," Jasmin said, slipping on her sunglasses.

Elric frowned as Torie slipped into her seat.

"That's not very comforting," he said, shutting Torie's door and waving to them as they pulled out.

"Whew, that man has it bad," said Jasmin, giving Torie a playful look.

She didn't say anything but was painfully aware of the hint of red that was no doubt creeping up her neck. She smiled. Elric wasn't the only one who had it bad.

"Is he okay?" asked Jasmin.

"What? Yeah of course. He's just going to miss me."

"No, not the wolf, your dragon," she said, nodding at Leo who had curled into a ball on Torie's lap.

Looking down, Torie could see the little dragon had his eyes closed and was snoring lightly. Tiny wisps of smoke unfurled from his nostrils as he snored lightly. The spiny ridge that ran down his back vibrated, running through a variety of colors from deep reds and oranges to bright greens and pinks.

"Huh. I've never seen him do that," said Torie. "He must sense that we are leaving him for a bit. We really haven't been separated since we got him."

"He's attuned to your emotions. So, I'm betting he is more worked up than usual because you are."

Torie pursed her lips and glanced at her friend. "Point taken. I really am looking forward to this. And thank you for suggesting it."

"Oh, you aren't the only one who needed a getaway. I haven't had a break in some time." She glanced at Leo and then Torie. "I hope he's going to be okay staying with Fionna while you're away."

"They get along great. He'll be just fine."

Hex and the Single Witch:
Chapter Two

He was, in fact, not fine at all.

If anything, Torie developed newfound admiration for Fionna's skill at wrangling an unhappy dragon. Leo cried and threw a tantrum like a toddler being left out of the fun stuff by their older siblings. He clung desperately to Torie, wailing incessantly, as Fionna tried to peel him off her.

Finally, she was able to lure him to her side with a slab of uncooked ribeye steak; that had Leo licking his tiny, sharp teeth; eyes wide in gluttony as he followed her back into her house. Torie and Jasmin waved to her as they backed out quickly before Leo could change his mind. Torie found herself hoping the little guy was all huff and puff and didn't burn Fionna's house down.

"Well, that was fun," Jasmin said.

"It just goes to show that I should socialize him more. Maybe spend time around other people with him before he gets…" She trailed off, not wanting to think about what she was going to do with a fully grown dragon as a pet.

"Before he gets big enough to eat someone?" Jasmin finished.

"Well, I wasn't thinking about it like that, but thank you for putting that image in my head."

"Next time we will go somewhere dragon friendly, so he can come along as well. And we will bring Fionna also. It feels weird not having her along."

Torie nodded. Even though they both knew Fionna needed to spend some time with her wife, Glen, it was tough not having her bubbly self tagging along for the ride.

"Well, I think we should establish some ground rules," Jasmin said.

"Such as?"

"Well, no talk about boyfriends. Or relationships. Or—"

Torie held up a hand to cut her off. "Wait, why do I feel like that is aimed solely at me?"

"Well, if the wolf fits...," said Jasmin. "And honestly, you know I love you, and you know I am...starting...to love Elric. But this weekend is about us relaxing and living life. Not him."

Torie didn't say anything as she pondered the rule.

"And you're not going to be able to do that, are you?" said Jasmin.

Torie laughed. "Well, how about if I promise to try my best?"

"Good enough."

"Then I have a rule as well," Torie quipped.

"Go for it."

"We can't just automatically say no to something just because it is outside of our comfort zone."

Jasmin offered her a sly glance. "Oh, you must be talking about you. Cos I know you're not trying to throw a jab at me."

Torie laughed. "Okay, Miss put-any-sauces-on-the-side-cos-I-don't-want-any-of-my-food-touching-any-of-my-other-food."

Jasmin pursed her lips and focused on the road ahead.

"Don't blame me because I like to enjoy the taste of my food without it being contaminated by the flavors of everything else on the plate," she replied.

They both laughed and then rode in silence for a bit before Torie spoke up.

"So, what is this place we are going to again? Where did you hear about it?"

"It's called Greenview Resort. It's supposed to be one of the best in the country. Five-star experience all the way around. Great food, spa...oh and naturally heated underground mineral baths. I can't wait. We are in for a long weekend of pampering."

Torie looked at the navigational screen in the center of the console that was leading them on their grand adventure.

"I've never been to West Virginia," she said. "Not even on a layover flight to anywhere."

"Well, it's not really on the way to anything. If you're going to West Virginia, it is the final destination."

"This is where you grew up, right?" Torie asked.

"The state, yes. But not where we are going. I grew up in the poor, mining communities in the southern part. Most of them are just ghost towns now, so there is nothing to go back to. But the central portion, where we are going, was always like some mythical Hollywood to me as a child; a place you always heard about but would never have the means to visit. So, when I heard about this world-renowned spa that opened there, I figured it would be the perfect getaway for us."

"Well, it looks like we are going to pass through a lot of

attractions on the way there. We can stop for some sight-seeing along the way."

Jasmin frowned, glancing at the clock.

"Maybe. But I don't want us getting there too late. It would be nice to walk the grounds some before it's dark."

Torie fiddled with the navigation system a bit more, scrolling through the list of interesting places to see, before clearing her throat and turning to Jasmin.

"You know, there is something I really think we need to talk about."

"Does it have to do with your pet...the dragon or the wolf?" She turned and flashed Torie a smile. "Sorry. Couldn't resist."

"Haha. No, it has nothing to do with either of them. It has to do with us."

"Oh? In that case, I'm listening."

"I've been thinking about what we found out... about us."

Torie could see the tension rise in Jasmin as she read-justed her hands on the steering wheel, gripping it slightly harder.

"And I can't figure out if what we were told was the truth or some elaborate lie," she continued.

"Well, I say look at the source it came from. That old shapeshifter was lying to us. It wanted to get into our heads and throw our game off."

"That's what I thought," said Torie. "But then, I wondered what they would get out of lying to us about that. But also, my mother adored you. Why would she do that if we were from two different, and warring, covens? Why would she have introduced us? And your mother never said anything about covens that shouldn't interact, right?"

Jasmin shook her head. "But my mother died well

before my magic kicked in. We never got to have any of those mother-daughter bonding moments."

Torie fidgeted with her seatbelt momentarily. "I went to the town hall to see what I could find out about our families."

Jasmin turned to face her briefly before returning her eyes to the road. "And?"

"Well, my old surname—Deadman—definitely wasn't one of the more popular names in the county. They were known for their secrecy and generally not the nicest family to get along with. I traced your name back as far as I could find it, but there is no hint of it in the records after a couple of generations."

"Probably because I didn't grow up here. As far as I know, I have no family in the region. We were all from West Virginia."

"That's what I was thinking. And I mean…well, since we are going to be in the state…" Torie let her voice trail off.

Jasmin let out a hard laugh that almost sounded more like a bark. "No way. I haven't been anywhere near my hometown in ages. Even if we made that drive, I can assure you there is nothing there that will be of any use to us. That place was dying when I left; I'm betting there isn't even a town hall anymore."

"But it wouldn't hurt to check. Plus, it's literally on the way to the resort," Torie said. "And just think, you can show me all the old places you used to play as a kid. Where you went to school, where you—"

"Okay, okay, I'll think about it. Maybe we can look at leaving the resort a little early and drive down there before heading back home."

Torie didn't say anything as she shrank back into the plush leather seat and stared out her window.

"Fine. But that means we have plenty of time to stop along the way for food." She rummaged around finding the paper bag Elric had presented her with. "Oh, we can have scones now."

"Uh-uh, missy. You put that back. You are not eating those greasy things in my car. That will be a snack when we pull over for gas."

Torie smiled as she pretended to pout. Something told her this was going to be a great little adventure they were headed on.

"There, now isn't this nicer than sitting in a gas station parking lot?" Torie said.

They were just over three hours into their road trip, and she had convinced Jasmin to take a forty-five-minute detour to an overlook along a mountain pass. The scenic beauty that spread out before them was unrivaled. The overlook was situated above a valley pass between two mountains, with the valley and meandering river flowing magically beneath them.

They sat on a picnic table enjoying their scones, as well as a basket of cheeses and cucumber sandwiches that Torie had made. The fresh, crisp, mountain air bit at their cheeks as the sun started its downward arch for the evening.

"I have to admit, this is breathtaking," said Jasmin. "I'm not sure it's a match for our mountain, but it's certainly up there." She stood up, stretched, and began gathering their things. "C'mon. We've lost time. If we don't make any more stops, we should get there just before the end of the day."

"Why are we in a hurry? What's so important about being there before sunset?" Torie asked.

"Well, if we're there before it gets dark, we can walk the grounds and see if we need to set up any protection wards."

Torie stopped just as she was packing the plates back into the picnic basket.

"Jasmin, why would we need wards? We are on vacation, remember?"

"Yes, we are on vacation, but we are not going to be stupid. There is mess everywhere, and you know it. Better we are prepared than caught off guard."

Torie stood there, her hands on her hips as she stared at her friend.

"Jas, this resort has been around for a few years now. It's populated by normal, everyday humans, having a perfectly normal time. I don't think we are going to need protection wards." She went back to packing the basket and then was struck by an idea. "Hey, what if we add another rule to our trip. A no-magics rule."

Jasmin looked at her, blinking her eyes almost comically before she started walking around slowly, looking down at the earth and scraping the toe of her shoe through the dust and grass.

"What are you looking for?" Torie asked.

"The rock you must have fell on and bumped your head," came the reply.

Torie couldn't help but laugh. "C'mon, I'm serious. We are trying to get out of Singing Falls for a couple of days. So, it should be physically *and* mentally. We leave the magic behind us for a few days. Besides, we don't want to attract attention."

"We are hex witches, Torie. We are going to attract

attention wherever we go. It just might not always be the humankind."

That was something Torie had been wondering about, and she made a mental note to ask Jasmin about it later, after their road trip. Had Singing Falls always been such a bizarre hot spot for supernatural activity gone wrong? Or had it all started after Torie had to move to town? And if so, why?

"Again, all we are agreeing to do is try our best to stick to a rule. This one doesn't have to be hard and fast either; but let's at least try."

Jasmin rolled her eyes but smiled and nodded. "Okay. But I'm telling you right now, if we get jumped by some hell demon and killed, I promise you my last words will be, 'I told you this was a stupid rule'."

Torie couldn't help but laugh as she finished packing up the basket. They dropped the trash in the nearby receptacle and climbed into the car.

"Okay, if we head back to the highway, we can just make it before sunset," Jasmin said, firing up the engine.

"Or," said Torie as she punched at the navigation screen. "We could take this road that winds through the mountains and enjoy the views." She pulled up an alternate route and pointed at the screen.

Jasmin frowned looking over the display. "It will definitely be dark once we arrive if we go that way."

"But we don't have wards to worry about now. Besides, I want to see the countryside."

Jasmin sighed, knowing she wasn't going to win this one. "Fine. But we better not get lost. It gets cold at night up here this time of year."

Torie nodded and settled back into the seat. She knew that her friend wasn't just giving in. She was enjoying the trip as well, and, just maybe, she was starting to relax a little.

With a sigh, Jasmin eased the Jaguar onto the road, turning away from the highway and towards the more scenic backroads that would take them to their destination.

One hour into the detour, and a half-hour after passing the last gas station in sight, the check engine light came on, followed by a lot of flashing lights on the dash, followed by the car locking up and crawling to a stop on the side of the deserted road.

Grab your copy...
vinci-books.com/singlewitch

About the Author

M.J. Caan is an avid reader and writer of all things science fiction and fantasy. Author of multiple science fiction and paranormal fantasy series, M.J. likes to think that there is still magic out there in the world. Even if it's only between the pages of a great book.